AF472667

# The Egypt in my Looking Glass

A Novella

Yuri Kruman

*AuthorHouse™*
*1663 Liberty Drive*
*Bloomington, IN 47403*
*www.authorhouse.com*
*Phone: 1-800-839-8640*



*Cover design by Margarita Korol of UrbanPopArtist.com*

*Author photo by Anna Chana Demidova of March13 Photography.*



*Published by AuthorHouse 12/31/2013*

*ISBN: 978-1-4918-4776-3 (sc)*

*Library of Congress Control Number: 2013923253*



*This book was made possible thanks to a generous grant by COJECO Blueprint Fellowship, The Genesis Philanthropy Group and UJA-Federation of NY.*

# Dedication

This book is dedicated with love and boundless—if never-quite-sufficient—gratitude to my dearest mother, Dr. Inna Kruman. Her kindness, dedication, sharp wit, fearsome intelligence and relentless humanity in the face of daunting challenges have been my guiding light since (before) birth. Her boldness is nothing short of Mosaic—in bringing her children out of our modern-day, *Soviet* Egypt, in raising them to be *menschen*, in educating them and in giving them a thoroughly better life in the Land of Streets Paved with (Not-Quite-) Gold. My success is a testament to the best training for life I can imagine—the Kruman Laboratory.

This book is also dedicated to Rivka Efrat (Jennifer), my wife and eshet hayil, an amazing mother to our daughter, my light and my everything. This book and many other things would have been quite impossible without her patience and support.

Lastly, but no less importantly, this book is dedicated to our daughter Leora, may she know no Egypt in her life, yet always remember the Exodus. By the time she can read this inscription, may she be living and thriving in her home, the land of Israel.

# Acknowledgments

"The Egypt In My Looking Glass" would be impossible without Jennifer, my wife, whose steadfast support, patience and foresight are my bedrock. An enormous debt of gratitude is owed to Dr. Inna Kruman, my mother, to whom I owe my life and my true education in this world, as well as our exodus from the *Soviet* Egypt.

This book was made possible thanks to a generous grant by COJECO Blueprint Fellowship, The Genesis Philanthropy Group and UJA-Federation of NY. The people (both staff and fellow fellows) I have met throughout my year as a Blueprint fellow have made for an incredibly enriching and inspiring experience throughout the writing process.

A huge thank you is reserved to my amazingly talented illustrator and editor, Margarita Korol (of UrbanPopArtist.com), and photographer, Anna Chana Demidova (of March13 Photography). Your great work makes having one's book judged by its cover distinctly palatable.

# 1

# Tolik

Tolik jumped out from his black Altima, incensed.

"You stupid fucker, you just hit me! What's your problem? Why did you cut me off? Where are you looking, idiot?"

"Fuck you. You cut me off, you bastard. It's *your* fault."

The Paki cabbie in his Pashtun garb was fierce. His dye-job-looking orange beard was bobbing as he yelled, "You pay me. There is damage."

"Fuck you, you Paki bastard. You're at fault. You're paying *me* for this. That's like $2K, at least," he lied.

"You fucking Jew, I pay you nothing! I will sue you."

"Not before I do, you Osama asshole. You ever heard of Weil & Manges? Well, you will. That's the best law firm in the world. My cousin will destroy your ass."

Things nearly came to blows on Coney Island Avenue and Brighton on a Monday morning. Police pulled up. The siren halted spittle, promises to knock out teeth, if not away at once. The officers were quick to urge restraint.

One took the lead. "Stand back. Calm down. You step away, Sir. And you too. What happened here?" A flood poured out from both.

"He hit me, officer."

"No, he hit *me*."

"Alright, not all at once. You Sir, is this your cab? And this, your Altima? Alright. I'm gonna ask you both to get back in your cars. Back in the car, Sir, yes. You need to move your cab down to the curb. Then put the car in Park and wait for Officer Dominguez. He'll need your license, registration. Have it ready. And your medallion number, too. Sir, please stop yelling and get going. Don't make me take you in and book you now. Yes, I will give you my badge number. First, move your cab please. *Now*." The cabbie cursed in Pashto and in Arabic and slammed his door shut.

Tolik operated calmly, getting in his car. Procedure was ingrained by now, from multiple encounters.

"License and registration, please." The officer twisted his face in knots, pronouncing without a clue. "A-na-to-ly. Anatoly. Yab-lon-ski. Mr. Yablonski, do you own this car?"

"Yes, officer, I do."

"Alright, tell me what happened here." He waited with his notepad ready. Tolik evaluated him. *South Bronx kid, probably not more than twenty-three*. His forearms glared with cluttered tats. One said "MARIA RIP," the other showing a large, bleeding heart and date, 11/5/09. At least the young man's fervor was in service of the law. One felt safe, only just. They boded well, recruits like this. Well, he was nice enough.

Tolik explained with well-feigned calm, "He came out from my left and cut me off when turning from the left lane on to Brighton. Crazy guy. He hit me on the front, trying to squeeze in. I need to get insurance info from this guy."

"Alright, Sir, just a second. He didn't show his turn before he hit you, nothing?"

"No. The cars from there go straight. I've lived here twenty years—I'd know."

"Uh-huh. And were you speeding?"

"Not at all! I was just parked there, at the stoplight, then I went on green."

"Alright. Sit tight."

Tolik observed the time. How long would this outrageous waste of time go on? It managed to be eight. He was already twenty minutes behind schedule. He dialed the receptionist.

"Hey, I'll be in late today. Some asshole cabbie hit me on the way. Police is here, it's taking time. Just a disaster. Can you call the nine o'clock and tell them I'll be late? Давай, красавица, I'll see you soon."[1]

---

1 Alright, gorgeous.

What stress relief, this girl. Ouwhee! He had her in his palm, too. She was from Bishkek and fresh. No papers, not a soul for family here. Just dropped down in his lap, responded to his ad. Sweet Lord, a body just to die for. Tolik drifted off.

The officer appeared. "Sir," Tolik bit his bottom lip, surprised. "Here's the insurance information."

"Fank you, offifer," he mumbled through the pain.

*Hamid Abdali. May he be entered from behind, in peace, the bastard.*

"Have a nice day, Sir."

"Thank you, officer. And you, as well." He rolled the window up and carried on. The anger simmered, but he let it go. He took off. Potap and Nastya blasted high, "И может быть про все забыть/И сердце мне открыть и душу отпустить/А может быть тебе про все сказать/ Ведь я не буду спать, если не буду знать."[2]

He pulled up to a building, Midtown Office Center under the Gowanus, up toward the water. He parked with great precision by the chain-link fence. Upon floor 2, he greeted client 1 quite curtly, asking for 5 minutes. Inside the room, marked with a lawyer's shingle, he sat down. He took out his Lenovo laptop from his backpack and began the day. After a couple clicks, Tolik picked up the phone and called in Masha over intercom. "Маша, вопрос вам. Можете зайти?"[3]

---

2 *And maybe I will forget everything/And open up my heart and let my soul on out?And maybe tell you everything/'Cuz I won't sleep, if I won't know.*

3 Masha, question for you. Can you come in?

He shut the door as she walked in. He grabbed her by the waist and pulled her in, kissing her strongly on the mouth and neck. Frazzled, protesting weakly, she gave in. He copped a feel, his hand now hiking up her skirt. Just as he felt her, wet and riled, the phone cut short the fun. She quickly straightened skirt, her hair and blouse. He signaled what would happen later and picked up.

“Алё? Да, Алик? Вы готовы? Приеду завтра к вам к шести. Пока.”[4] He found the Purell bottle, spurting out, with doctor’s motion to apply all over, carefully—not to miss a spot. “Окей. Увидимся. Платеж мой не забудьте, а? Две тысячи, мы договаривались. Ладно, до завтра.” [5] He hung up, texting Masha, “send him in.”

The client knocked and was invited in. Tolik collected papers from the table quickly, throwing pile on chair.

“Да, проходите. Костя?”[6]

“Да.”

“Чем я могу помочь вам?”[7]

“Ваш друг Сережа Мельник вас порекомендовал.”[8] This Kostya had a sorry accent. *Born here or came young.*

---

4 Hello? Yeah, Alik? Are you ready? I’ll be over tomorrow at 6. Bye… Ok, see you. Don’t forget my payment, ok? Two thousand, as agreed. Alright, until tomorrow.

5 Ok, we’ll see each other. Don’t forget my payment. Two thousand, as we agreed. Alright, until tomorrow.

6 Yeah, come in. Kostya?

7 How can I help you?

8 Your friend Seryozha Melnik recommended you.

"Alright, so what is it you want my help with? Let's get right to the point."

"Oh, well, he said you know some people that do treatments after accidents."

"Wait, you're the lawyer with your own new office out on Emmons, right?"

"Yep, that's me."

"You do PI, med mal, all that assorted shit, correct?"

"Yeah, that's my bread and butter."

"Alright, I get the picture. I got what you need. Hey Kostya, you know Weil and Manges?"

"You're probably referring to Weil, Gotshal, right?"

"Yeah, it's a long name." he waved off. "I got a cousin who's a partner there. We are close like *this*." Tolik raised index and the middle finger, lingering with emphasis.

"Partner at Weil?! Damn, that's hot shit. What is his name?"

"Don't worry, you don't need to know. But let's just say he's taught me quite a lot. You have to know, you're dealing with someone who knows his craft."

"And that I see." Kostya was thoroughly impressed.

"Partner at Weil. That's crazy shit, bro."

"Don't *bro* me. We don't know each other."

Kostya threw up his palms. "I'm sorry, you are right. All business."

"Alright. Now listen up. I need to know that I can trust you. Give me references."

"You want my references?!"

"You heard me right. Don't waste my time. I have my way of doing business. Do it or goodbye."

"Alright. How about Seryozha?"

"One is not enough. Three is my minimum."

"Wow, three, ok. I'll get you three."

"Professional, need two. Serge can be personal for you."

"I can't believe this. What's so special that you offer?"

Tolik sat up, assuming salesman mode. He rattled off, "our network has forty-three practices around Midwood, Flatbush, Brighton and Coney Island, even Cobble Hill and Carroll Gardens. Our agents cover all the Brooklyn hospitals. There is no guarantee, but our clients do see an average intake of five more plaintiffs every month. Some see as many as 10 more. That is 120 for the year. Average settlement, $10K. You get a third, $3K, a little more. That's revenue of $360K a year, on top of what you take in now, which—judging by your presence here—is little."

"I'll have to check these numbers with your references."

My dearest Kostya. What shitty, Tier 3 law school did you go to that you ask such things? To Pace or CUNY Queens or what? You sure you passed the bar? Maybe I need to check, myself? Don't waste my time. The door is open. Ciao."

"Alright, alright, relax. Just asking. Yes, I was admitted just four months ago."

"No jobs out there—it's tough, I know."

"Yeah, man, it's hard. Got loans like crazy. Gotta feed the wife and kid."

"A girl or boy?"

"A boy."

"Cute. What's his name?"

"Misha."

"That's nice. I got a cousin Misha on my father's side."

"Listen, ok. I got the rules. How much is this subscription service gonna cost me?"

"Don't get your panties in a wad. Half."

"Half what? Half of my net?"

"Get the fuck out of here. Half of your revenues from us. Take or leave it, *bro*."

"Half of the revenue, and *I* do all the work? You've got some balls, man. Are you fucking crazy?"

"Business is business. That's our fee."

"Yeah, I don't think so. That's insane."

"Look, think it over. $180K a year, a hundred after tax. You could repay your loans—$100K, 2 years, quite easily. You'll have your life back, treat your wife. It's a sweet deal. You won't need to look half the day for clients. You're a smart guy. Don't waste this chance. Nobody has my kind of reach. I know you know that or you wouldn't come."

Kostya looked up, breathed out the last of red flag reservations, nodding.

"You've made a smart choice, Kostya. You will see." Tolik stood up and reached his hand out. Kostya false-grinned and shook his hand. "Alright, this is what happens now. My secretary—Masha—will explain logistics and draw up the paperwork. Don't worry, there's no funny business. We know *all* the rules." He pressed the intercom. "Masha, please take care of our client, Kostya. He'd like to work with us." To Kostya, "We will be in touch."

They nodded, parting, Kostya still internalizing. Tolik swung back to his workstation, pumping fist. This revenue was sorely needed. Good start to the week. Hey, not too shabby for a porn webmaster with a Kingsborough degree. Maybe not quite Weil-Manges levels of prestige and class—or money—but not bad, at all. By his last count, he had $200K saved up, small equity investments in 3 parking lots, a Merrill Lynch account and a Miami condo, wisely bought at auction in 2008. Compared to cousin Marik, with his useless Brown degree—one more poor writer with no future, he was downright flush.

Borka was situated well, it seemed. What was the Little Shit—his "rabbi"—up to? It was time to pay a call. But first, he needed to tie up loose ends.

"*Alo, Vassily Rosenberg,* please."

"Yes, one moment. May I ask who's calling?"

"Dr. Yablonskiy, Anatoliy."

"Hold one moment, please."

He twirled a pen in his left hand, awaiting patiently his sorry debtor."

"Ало? Доктор Яблонский? Вы откуда?"[9]

"Это я, болван. Всего-лиш Толик."[10]

"Ах, Толик."[11] A sigh of fear went not unnoticed.

"Послушай, Вася, я приеду к вам в четверг, в часиков пять, забрать что я забыл на той неделе. Приготовтесь."[12]

"А, да, конечно. Мы все приготовим. Извините, дорогой."[12]

"Предупреждаю вас, это последний раз. В следующий, я точно не забуду."[13]

"Да да, конечно, не волнуйтесь. Все готово."[14]

---

9 Hello? Dr. Yablonskiy? Where are you calling from?

10 It's me, you fool. Just Tolik.

11 Oh, Tolik.

12 Listen, Vasya (Vassily), I'll be over on Thursday, around 5, to get what I forgot last weel. Be ready.

He hung up. He could just feel the panic spreading at the office, in the wake. Tolik rather enjoyed the formal address from an older, more accomplished man. Sometimes in this unruly and informal jungle—business—order and respect were needed, even indispensable. That it was in his favor hardly spoiled the pot. One had to take what was one's own. There was no instance when the prize arrived on silver, bound by lace.

On down the list. *"Dima, privet.* Yo, how was Vegas, bro? Was bitchin', right? You stayed at Wynn, just like I told you? Goood. You did Jean-George and Spearmint Rhino, didn't you? I know you, Dima. So predictable. One of these times, you gotta make it into XS, man. Might even have to dress—and not a little—classy. Ha!" Dima protested on the other end. "Alright, alright. Glad you enjoyed it, man. Next time, I'll show you all the hidden stuff, myself. Maybe for Labor or Columbus Day, we'll see. Listen, I'm calling to find out if you have news from that Nikita guy. It's been a while. We need an answer, like a month ago. Are they still into it or what? We're asking for a million, five. That's like their profit for one day. The deal is foolproof, man. The brownstone's under market price. Now with the ruling for Columbia, it's gonna spike in value. Easy profit. You know all this already, man. Can you just call him one more time? Tell him we have the papers ready, references and appraisal—even two. What do they want more, anyway? Just make it happen, bottom line. And if you know of others like Nikita out in Moscow, call them too, ASAP. I told you, if we get the money, close within a month, six weeks. We'll get out quarter-mil between us. It's not hard."

"Do you know anyone with money there, in Moscow?"

"*Me*?! Naah, man. We moved like twenty years ago, almost. Everyone's out of there a while. My uncle's there, but he's a scientist. He's lucky just to own his place. But money? Там не пахнет. [13] Look, try Nikita, think of friends or cousins, anyone. Even just $5K or $10K—anything's helpful. And when we make this deal, there will be others. *Davai*, let's make this happen, bro. Listen, I'm gonna see you out at Russian Vodka Room for Zhenya's birthday, right? Alright, bro, make it count. Peace out."

This oily weasel was annoying him—Nikita. What he would give not to rely on him or give him 10%. You dealt with Russians in their homeland, then you had to pay. It's either bribe the whole, entire fucking crew or just abandon ship. At least he could rely on Dima, even with his whoring. Baby Boy made it rain from trees, G-d bless him. That's what counted.

Tolik slinked back. He flicked his tongue with satisfaction. Not half bad. Things were beginning to look up. The last two years had given him a vicious beating. One, two, three, four—no, five; wait, six—his ventures all blew up like dominoes. He crossed his fingers, arteries and veins, *tfu tfu*, this thing with Russia would work out and maybe even Kostya. He would see. If even one panned out, he'd give up all the piecemeal coding jobs and app design, the small-time shit and focus on the big fish—his idea with Igor. Together with his "little" cousin a genius FOB, they planned to build sophisticated trackers for the movement

---

13 Doesn't even smell like it (money) there.

of large stocks, indexing Twitter, EDGAR filings, sales by management, plus major FX movements, supply chain participants and more. He planned to involve Boris once the code was tested, before launch. His one insider would do wonders even with his memos and an ear to ground. For now, Alyosha—wunderkind, with his two words of English—was just getting started. Hope against hope, with help from a big quant or two on Wall Street, they would hit it big.

It managed to be lunchtime before long. Tolik took off for Grandma Yufa's house. He stopped by NetCost Market for some groceries and parked around the corner, slogging up with bags.

"Бабуля, здравствуй! Это Толик, внук твой."[14]

"А? Кто это?"[15]

"Толик! Открой!"he screamed.[16]

"Толик?! А, Толик!" The chain now dangled futilely, a while. At last, the sliding sound. Success! His Baba Yufa stood there in her *tapochki*[17] and *sarafanchik*,[18] staring. Her eyes were gone with cataracts, her hearing barely on a thread. And still, she was determined at her 88.

The woman was a living wonder. She'd gone through

---

14 Granny, hello! It's Tolik, your grandson.

15 Ha? Who is it?

16 It's Tolik! Open up!

17 Slippers

18 House dress

husband #1 and later, 2, Great Patriotic War, miscarriage, one child's death, Stalin, Khrushchev and Brezhnev, emigration, even hurricane. Tolik and Babushka were close. One wrinkled and one dented pea, they'd clung together through the horrid and the bad. She was a second mother—often, first—at once a fragile creature and eternal.

Tolik put down the groceries on the kitchen table. "Ты что, сынок? Зачем мне эта вся еда? Ведь хом-эттэндентша пошла мне только покупать."[19]

"Да ладно, не волнуйся. Будет про запас. Как самочувствие?"[20]

"Да, так себе. Все бок болит, то зуб. Не видео ничего, бабка твоя. И слышит вот едва-едва. Передвигаться трудно. Так, тфу-тфу."[21]

"Ну, слава Б-гу. Как хом-эттэндентша? Новая, да?"[22]

"Да, Ванда. Ничего, пока. Полячка. Готовит ничего. Лучше чем прошлая, хотя-бы. Та своровала серебро, пропала. Сволочь."[23]

---

19 What for, my son? What for do I need this food? My home attendant just left to get me some.

20 It's alright, no big deal. You'll have it for later. How are you feeling?

21 Eh, so-so. My side hurts, then my tooth. Can't see a thing, your Granny. And hearing's really so-so. It's hard to move around. Otherwise, knock on wood.

22 Well, thank G-d for that. How is the home attendant? New one, right?

23 Yeah, Vanda. She's alright, so far. She cooks not badly. We." See. Better than that last one, at least. That one stole silver, disappeared. That bitch.

"Ладно. Так, вот тебе принес новый сел фон. А вот творог, кефир, овсянка, рыба свежая—лосось, сметана, черный хлеб, морковка, сельдерей, картошка. А вот тебе пихтовое масло и любимая газета—Русский Базар."[24]

"Ну, даешь! Ты слишком щедрый, Толенька. Будь осторожен, а то схватит там какая-то бабень."[25]

"Да, не волнуйся, Баба. Справлюсь, как-нибудь."[26]

"Садись, я накормлю."[27]

"Спасибо, с удовольствием."[28]

She took out the worn pot of soup, procured the ladle and a bowl and carefully doled out the lumpy, beet-stained liquid. Since childhood, he would wait all year to taste Grandma's cold summer soup—eggs, beets, cucumbers, radishes. Out came the sour cream and Borodinskiy bread. This was just heaven. He kissed his Baba Yufa on the left cheek with aplomb.

"Бабуля, ты даешь. Ты знаешь как люблю твой суп. Ну, просто кайф."[29]

---

24 Alright. I brought you a new cell phone. Here's farmer's cheese, kefir, oatmeal, fresh fish—salmon, sour cream, black bread, carrots, celery, potatoes. And here's your pine oil and favorite rag—Russian Bazaar.

25 You're really something! You're too generous, my little Tolik. Thank you. Watch out now, some rough woman might just grab you.

26 Don't worry, Granny. Will manage, somehow.

27 Sit, I will feed you.

28 Thnk you, with pleasure.

29 Granny, you're something else. You know how much I love your soup. It's just *beyond*.

"Ешь, ешь, сынок. Поменьше говори. Сейчас дам тебе котлетки и картошечку. Заморим червячка."[30]

He put aside the bowl, sat back, inhaling bliss. Simple and homemade was the best. The microwave went off. Baba brought out the steaming platter, the same she'd left with from the mother country. Old Soviet issue beat the new Chinese, hands down. He juggled the first bite between his lips and tongue. Best in the land, these chicken cutlets, then the boiled potatoes with their dill and sour cream.

Grandma sat down again. She held her hip in pain and *Oy*-ed. The life came back to her all-knowing hazel eyes.

"Ты полысел, мой дорогой."[31]

"Ну что-ж, бывает."[32] It was true. His sink and tub were witnesses. Age was no happiness, indeed.

"И вес набавил, кажется."[33]

"Не может быть. В серьез?"[34] He sat up, now alarmed. He grabbed his gut, then handles. *Shit.*

"Будь осторожен. Ты любишь есть и выпить, это точно."[35]

---

30 Eat, eat, my son. Talk less. Don't choke. I'll give you cutlets and potatoes. We'll *busy the worm* [have a good snack].

31 You've become bald, my dear.

32 Well… Happens.

33 And gained some weight, it looks like.

34 Can't be. For real?

35 Be careful. You'r eoine who likes to eat and drink, that's for sure.

"Just wait for it," he droned.

"Пора жениться," he intoned in time with Babushka. [36] Without an appetite, he swallowed last potato pieces and begged out for work. *There's your free lunch*, he thought. At least there were no questions of his love life.

"Циц. Сладенькое дам." [37]

"Да нет, не надо. Не могу." He knew Perdition Road, insisting no. [38]

"Так, подожди минутку. Просьба есть к тебе одна. Мне Климов выписал статин какой-то. Можешь взять?" [39]

"Конечно, да. Возьму." [40]

"Сейчас, найду." [41] She went into her room. Tolik sat down.

The room smelled musty, but familiar. Old, heavy Soviet blankets, wall rug, clock, the photos on the wall—a youthful Grandpa Syoma in his handsome prime. It was the greatest comfort, just to sit, remember all the gatherings and toasts, and most all, the stories from the war and later, Moscow. He had been deeply sentimental as a child. Life circumstances beat it out—and well. No use being wistful, anyway.

---

36 It's time to marry.

37 Wait, there's something sweet for you.

38 Oh no, no thanks. I can't.

39 Wait, just a moment. Just one favor. Klimov prescribed for me some *statin*. Can you get it?

40 Of course, yes, I will take it.

41 One second, let me find it.

He heard the rustle of some papers, looking at his watch. Already 1. Time to make scarce.

"Бабушка Юфа!" Nothing doing. *Let her do her thing.*

He looked ahead into the china cabinet. There was the precious samovar—pre-World-War-I, Czech crystal and East German dishes, then of course, the Soviet issue silver, tarnished, but in velvet case. And then the bookshelf—gloried treasure—with its sets of Chekhov, Pushkin, Lermontov, Tolstoy, Sholom Aleikhem and Balzac, Cervantes and Shakespeare—all the good old. People—his mother, uncles—had once read these volumes for edification; now, they had no audience. In Moscow childhood, he was drawn and racked with poetry and prose. The emigration mostly threw the parents off his scent. They had enough, their own big problems, then *kaput*! went marriage, right before their eyes. Pa couldn't handle starting over and went solo, damned be all of them, He up and met a woman, moved to Israel with her. Thanks, asshole, for support and love. And which was worse, it wasn't clear—original or second try. No wonder, Grandma's house was Eden.

Tolik sighed. All this accounting left a bitter taste. Even adulthood didn't heal some wounds. Would he be better as a husband? *Likely story.* The women he put up with were a sharp-toothed lot; the ones he dates, *oyoyoy.* But yes, he had to marry soon. He felt the marrow draining—slowly, but for sure. Maybe the next one, if she passed the test drive.

"На Толик, вот тебе. Ты можешь им отправить, на иншуренс?"[42]

"Ой, черт, совсем забыл."[43] He quickly found his wits and thought of the duty to report his accident.

"Что?" she asked, alarmed. [44]

"Да ладно, ничего. Просто забыл. Мне самому надо послать там коке-что."[45]

"Давай, сынок, иди. Все в добрый час. Найди себе невесту."[46]

"Ну, так и быть, найду. К тебе приведу."[47]

"Вот так, давай."[48]

"Давай, Бабуля. Ты сокровище мое. Заеду опять скоро, может с Мамой."[49]

"Скажи ей позвонить мне."[50]

---

[42] Here you go, Tolik. And also, can you drop this letter to the insurance company?

[43] Oh crap, I totally forgot.

[44] What is it?

[45] Ah, nothing special. Just forgot. I need to send something somewhere.

[46] Alright, son, go. All in good time. Go find yourself a bride.

[47] Well, if I must. You've got a deal. I'll bring her here to meet you.

[48] That's right. Good. Go.

[49] Granny, be well. You are my treasure. I'll come by soon, maybe with Mom.

[50] Tell her to call me.

He bent down to his Grandma's level, kissing her on cheek. She blessed him and he left. G-d bless her; she was fragile. Her fingers shook a little with the pour. She limped and wasn't in command, as usual. At 88, how could there be complaint? Her time was coming, he could feel. *Make time to see her, fool*, he thought.

He drove back, sullen, with the agent on the phone. He wasn't in the mood to argue or complain. "I'll get the estimate and fax it. Yes, by Friday. Thanks." Without a mind, he turned on BQE and cursed. The traffic was its lunchtime worst. He blasted Biggie's anthem. Oh yes, he liked it to be called Big Poppa.

After two verses, he flipped off, disgusted. Shit, he was turning 34 next week. What losers played this music at his age? Most all his classmates were long married with two babies and a solid job. And here he was, still hustling daily like a slave. He pounded with a string of curses on his steering wheel. Where had the time gone, with his youth? When did he grow into a bitter, balding, half-baked failure with no humor?

His temples tense, he swerved off at the exit, Ocean Parkway. He parked down by the water, walking just to clear his head. The people and the places were oppressing him, smiling and smirking, witnessing his slide. How many nights he'd wasted in his twenties here… Tatyana's, Oleandr, Golden Sphinx, the swimming delicacy piles, the pricy T&A!

The vomit of his booze-filled flashbacks colored everything. What he would give to clean the slate, start over elsewhere, without hustling, to take his Mother out of here! Borka was fine alone, hard-headed fool. Maybe LA, Miami, anywhere with sun and water, just not here. The hurricane was just another nail. But then, exactly how? How would he live, make money? Take debt, go back to school at almost 35? No way in hell. The reinvention thing was once a lifetime. His happened twenty years ago. The harvest was as such, and nothing more.

Of course, his uncle—paragon of brilliance—Edou-aard, had tried his hand at number 2, and look! Not only had he been a family man—3 kids!—then single, free again, become a famous scientist—respected, now a dissident. Some guys had all the luck—and brains and patience, incidentally, too. Alas.

Damn it to hell, what was this weakling shit about? Just yesterday, he was so high, out with his Masha, Gena and his chick, Regina, at some fair in Williamsburg. His hit parade of jokes at lunch—no, *brunch*—was excellent, pure genius; his take on lattes, bad tattoos and hipster frames—relentless. These people truly were repugnant, silly, head-in-ass. What did they know of work, these trustafarians, or failure, misery or joy? Their *shadows* were ironic; even *that* caused fear. He—Tolik—could explain to them with trembling pleasure how the world worked; the pillars—force, ambition, money, image—unassailable. To bother was to toss fair pearls at swine.

The sun peeked out from underneath the clouds. He smiled—he was still young and vigorous, with lots to prove. He bounded with a start, taking a jog back up the Boardwalk to his car. Tolik was winded. Time to hit the gym again.

Mom rang. "Да, Мам, привет. *Что слышно?*"[51]

"Толенька, слушай. Нас Рита приглашает в воскресение—день рожденья у нее."[52]

"Какая Рита? Не припоминаю."[53]

"Ну, тетя тебе, как-бы. Мама Марика и Вовы и Аллы."[54]

"А, Горелик. Правда?! Что случилось? Кого там наградили призом в этот раз?"[55]

"Да ладно тебе, просто приглашает. И Борьку и тебя."[56]

"А может тоже твоего Азария?"[57]

"Так, хватит. Дело не твое. Она сказало именно, ‹Толика, Борьку приводи.'"[58]

"А что, мы дети, нам нельзя самим сказать?"[59]

"Да ладно тебе, что ты все намылился? Просто не

---

51 Yeah Mom, what's up?

52 My little Tolik.listen. Rita's inviting us on Sunday—it's her birthday.

53 Which Rita? Don't remember any.

54 Well, she's an aunt to you, they say. The mother of Marik and Vova and Alla.

55 Oh, Gorelick. Really? What happened? Who won an award this time?

56 Pipe down. She's just inviting us. Both Borka and you.

57 And maybe your Azary, too?

58 Enough. It's not your business. She said specifically bring Tolik and Borka.

59 So what, we're still like kids? She can't tell us herself?

знает телефонов ваших, вот и все. Так значит, будешь или нет?"[60]

"Посмотрим. Планы есть уже. Зачем мне это нужно, сверху вниз смотрели чтобы на меня? Все из себя, подумаешь."[61]

"Ты не забудь, мой дорогой, как Вова тебя спас однажды, и как Алла за тобой смотрела в детстве. И Марик кстати тоже, тебе братик. Забыл, как вы играли дружно в детстве там и Бабушки. Совесть имей. Прийди."[62]

"Ладно, увидим. А Борька, наш раввин, прийдет? "[63]

"Прийдет."[64]

"Соскучился, давно не видел. Ладно, постараюсь."[65]

"Давай, бегу. Потом поговорим."[66]

"Окей. Приеду в шесть, после работы."[67]

---

60 Calm down. Why are you all worked up? She just doesn't know your numbers, that's it. So, will you come or not?

61 We'll see. Already have some plans. Why do I need this, to be looked down upon? They're all so full of themselves.

62 Don't forget, my dear, how Vova saved you once and Alla baby-sat you as a kid. And Marik, also, is your brother. Forgot how you used t play so well together at Granny's? Have some decency. Show up.

63 Alright, we'll see. And Borka—our dear rabbi—will he be there?

64 Yes, he will.

65 I miss him. Haven't seem him in forever. Alright, I'll try.

66 Good. I have to run. Talk later.

67 Ok, I'll be over at 6, after work.

"Азарий будет пол восьмого, в восемь."[68]

"Как раз, поем и смоюсь."[69]

"Целую. Bye."[70]

"Пока."[71]

Pfff, cousins. What the hell. How many years since he had seen them last? 4? 5? Shit, time was ruthless. He was 29 back then. How many lifetimes had he shed since then? Let's see. He was with Vika then, love of his life. The effing bitch took his best years. He was odd-jobbing then, website design, coding for hire, still in The Biz. Maybe not strange that Vika left him, after all. What half-respectable nice girl would want to deal with that? "*What does your boyfriend do?*" "*Odd jobs and porn.*" At least this stage was over, long ago. G-d bless them at a distance, all those "people," crooks and saints, the kingpins and the lowly pawns. Good riddance, actually. That's it, one more good deal gone through, and out. Clean break, an honest living. Word of honor.

So, cousins. Well, alright. They may be snobs, with all their fancy jobs and condos and all that, but they had interesting lives. Worst he could do was listen and enjoy the meal. The food was always excellent at Rita's. *Well, that's that.*

Back at the office, Tolik eschewed conversation. Masha

---

68 Azariy will be there at seven thirty, eight.

69 Perfect, I'll eat and get on out.

70 Kiss you.

71 Bye.

turned shameless, he could see. Chatting away like a bazaar girl on the phone, she sat there, painting nails. No longer did she even feign activity in front of him. This would not, simply could not stand. He'd whip her into shape, the lazy bitch. But not right now.

He shut himself away. There were new leads on properties to check, all those "big people" to contact and wine and dine. But frankly, he was hard up for the effort just to chat and flatter, coax and denigrate himself. Two projects in the pipeline wasn't bad.

Tolik, The Hacker, went to work. Alla Gorelik—maiden name intact. A picture of her boys on Facebook. *Director, Inbound Marketing at Pfizer.* Damn. Married to Ari Goldman, *Managing Director at Apollo.* Holy shit. Alright. And Vlad Gorelik? *Associate, Bankruptcy Litigation.* Wait, *associate?!* Hadn't he worked in law for 8—or was it 10?—years now? Well, that just sucked. Wife, Dina Greenberg at Ogilvy Mather, an Associate Director. Wow, ok. And Mark Gorelik—*author, blogger, editor, Atlantic Wire.* Fancy. First novel to be published next year, spring.

What would be his excuse? Business Development? Fund-raising? Human Capital? CEO/President of AmRus Enterprises? That's pathetic, bleh. He ran a startup incubator, *that* was it!

Tolik was drifting, lost in thought. Before he could object much, it was five. The afternoon was shot. In one last act of salvaged relevance, he called in Masha.

"Keep the door open," he now ordered. "Masha, sit down."

Sensing a shit storm of assertion, she obeyed. "Let me be clear. I won't repeat myself. Why are you here?"

"Because I work."

"That's right. You're here to work. I'm paying you good money *not* to paint your nails, *not* chat all day, *not* waste your fucking time and mine. If I see <u>one</u> more time how you behaved yourself today, I'll throw you out. Bye, bye. Now, is that clear?"

"But..."

"But nothing. Yes or no."

"Yes."

"That is all."

With puppy eyes that dripped with sex, she muttered. "Толик, погоди."[72]

*"Enough. Good night. Go home."*

Seeing no headway, Masha shrank away and left. He bit his bottom lip with vicious force, then clamped his teeth. These things were necessary, time to time. He took his backpack with him, locked up and left. He made some calls to ease the guilt, while stuck on BQE. He let himself in up at Mom's, threw down his bag, unbuttoning his shirt. Not to confuse, he shouted out his presence. Mom acknowledged from a "special place." Dragged by the day, Tolik was tired. He yawned spectacularly, then spread-eagled back into the

---

72 Tolik, wait.

couch. He dabbed his tearing eyes and made out the disused piano, up against the wall. How many years it was, since he last played, he wondered? Rust was awful.

An almost childish urge took over. He had to feel the keys, to play—or try, at least. My G-d, what an embarrassment! His digits had long atrophied. He threw the crocheted rag right off the cover, opened and began to stretch his fingers out. There was a time… He even was not bad, at all. Mom had a great technique and taught him steadfastly, for years. Three, often four a day, the practices! How did he have the discipline, back then? The discipline had him, more to the point. It seemed like three, four lives ago. These twenty years had run with shameless speed, like silent film stills through an empty room. And where, for what? He practiced passages from notes in air—Chopin's Third Nocturne—first he saw. His finger memory revived, chord after cringing chord. Even some sort of rhythm appeared. Tolik ran through the solemn first four bars.

"Too fast. Slow down." Mom was behind him. *Pressure!* Nerves kicked in, like recital-day. He stumbled badly once, then twice, regrouped, took a deep breath, resolved to nail it. He found his poise and straightened up his back. The seat needed adjustment. He obliged. *Technique*! Wrists up, straight back, up on the bench.

The third time, he began with undue energy, withdrew, adjusted, winced at the badly tuned low notes. He worked his way back up with care, up wave and back. He held back, then worked up with zeal, crescendo with nobility—not terror—then again, to depths.

The spark was there, by G-d! But yes, inflections lost completely and performer's measuredness. Somehow… this piece was not for show, took patience he could hardly muster. Etudes were easier. Oh well.

"Сынок, ты что—соскучился?"[73]

"Да нет. Бывает. Просто захотелось. Что-то осталось с детства."[74]

"Да, наверно. Все от учителя зависит." Ira winked.[75]

"Помнишь как заставляла все играть, играть, часами? Больше не могу!"[76]

"Упрямый сын, однако, у меня."[77]

"Сама такая. Вся семейка."[78]

They could only laugh. They left the normal platitudes on stand-by, moving to the kitchen. She had made голубцы—his favorite. He ate with lusty, hurried appetite, relieved by knowing silence. Ira could only grin. Her eldest wasn't irritated and enjoyed. *Tfu tfu*, he looked more energized than usual, even sentimental. What got him, she could only wonder. Mama or some girl? Was she intelligent and decent,

---

73 Son, what is the matter? Do you miss it?

74 Naah, happens. Just wanted to play. Something has stayed since childhood.

75 Yeah, I bet. All depends on your teacher.

76 Remember how you used to make me play and play, for hours? I can't, anymore!

77 A stubborn one, I have, it's true.

78 Takes one to know one. Ourwhole family.

hopefully? No use, as always, asking for details. Time for a wife and children. *Soon…*

He finished wiping up the sauce with bread. "Спасибо, Мам."[79]

"Ну как, наелся?"[80]

"Да, спасибо. Очень вкусно."[81]

"Ну, я рада. Возьми арбуз, сынок."[82]

"Пожалуй да, возьму."[83]

She brought him slices from the fridge.

"Как раз, точно что надо."[84]

"Бери, бери, давай."[85]

Tolik refreshed his palate happily, observing. Mom wasn't getting any younger—59, this year—but she was undiminished. Between her fast outrage at news—Сволочи! Гады! Террористы! [86]– and her criticism of woman, man

---

79 Thanks, Mom.

80 Alright, you're sated?

81 Yes, thank you. Very tasty.

82 Well, I'm glad. Take watermelon, son.

83 Why not? I will.

84 Exactly what was needed.

85 Take, take.

86 Sons of bitches! Vipers! Terrorists!

and President—"Мы знаем эти штуки все. Гнать надо, поскорее!"[87]– she was her vibrant self, full stop. *Thank G-d.*

Tolik was late. He tendered leave, blinking his eyes, head bowed.

"Беги, сынок. Ты будешь в воскресение? К Рите едем?"[88]

"Ну да, уже. Уговорила."[89]

She kissed him on the cheek, her *malchik*, noting with her eyes his pate. At least no grey yet. That arrived late throughout her line.

"Не забудь Бабушке лекарство."[90]

"Ой черт. Ну ладно, сейчас зайду. Пока."[91]

He popped by Walgreens, dropping off prescription and rode home. Why had he stopped piano studies? What a pity. Maybe he'd start again. Just let the payday come, and soon!

In general, he'd slipped. There was a time when he had gone to Met a handful times a year, ballet once in a while. No time, must hustle, make a living. Somewhere along the golden trail, the carriage had detoured to fix a wheel,

---

87 We know these tricks from long ago. It's long been time to chase this guy from office!

88 Get going, my son. Will you be there on Sunday? Are we going to Rita's?

89 Alright, already. You convinced me.

90 Don't forget the medication for Grandma.

91 Oh, crap. Alright, I'll go over now. Bye.

avoid the deluge, and replace the axle. That was that. And in the end, one wondered, quite unthinkably, the worth of the uprooting, all things equal. Look at his Moscow cousins, not so badly off—at all. Whose propaganda was the stronger and whose truth?

Back home, he freshened up and dressed. Gena was coming over after 9 to ride to the West Village, to Onegin. Tolik was itching for a drink or five. He'd ride the bitch seat for the night. *Whatever.* He picked out his best party shirt—pale purple, bluish, his fake Diesel jeans, Armani Mania, his hipster wingtips. He was set.

Tolik hopped into Gena's new Infiniti Q50 and they rolled. The sun was setting gorgeously, the ocean glistening with summer. Depeche Mode was the choice of poison, like in high school. By habit, they began to sing. "*Now I'm not looking for absolution/Forgiveness for the things I do./But before you come to any conclusions/Try walking in my shoes/Try walking in my shoes./You'll stumble in my footsteps. Keep the same appointments I kept./If you try walking in my shoes.*" They didn't need a word. The music managed all the talking; they'd known each other for too long for updates.

They parked fortuitously on West 10th, for once. Outside, a bitchy blonde and brunette friend were smoking; these two were FOB from Moscow, by the sound of it, both tall and confident, well-trained—and yet soliciting, de facto. Gena stepped up and pulled out cigs, offering Tolik, who was game. They lit up. Gena started.

*"Devushki, izvinitye, vi zdyes chasto? Mi zdyes perviy raz. Obichno mi tusuyemsya tam v Mari Vannye. Kak vam zdyes?"* [92]

The blonde acknowledged him just barely, late-turning with a look of practiced condescension. Odessa brogue plus unfamiliar lines were hardly helpful.

*"Akh da, vi v Mari Vannye chasto? Chestno vas ne pripominayu."* [93]

*"Gena. Eto Tolik."* [94]

*"Sveta. Eto Dasha."* [95]

*"Priyatno poznakomitsa."* [96]

*"Vzaimno."* [97]

The girls gave looks one to another, more or less, "w*hy not?*" The darker one put out her cigarette just thusly, eyeing Tolik with well-worn detachment. Sveta followed.

*"Mi mozhem poukhazhivat za vami, mademoiselles?"* [98] Gena was really on a limb, but hell, why not?

The ladies didn't answer no. The cue was set. Gena put

---

92 Ladies, our apologies. Are you here often? We're here for the first time. We're usually hanging out at Mari Vanna. How do you find this place?

93 It's true, you're in Mari Vanna often? Quite honestly, I don't remember you.

94 Gena. This is Tolik.

95 Sveta. This is Dasha.

96 Pleasure to meet you.

97 It's mutual.

98 May we look after you this evening, mademoiselles?

out his cig and set his hunting eyes on blonde. Tolik was not averse; their preferences dovetailed neatly. He took a puff—one last—and went to work. They sat down at the bar, paired up. The girls insisted to speak English only, for their practice.

Gena and Tolik nodded to each other, clever boys.

"What do you do?" the girls both asked at once, raising their voices over music.

"We work together. We do real estate."

"Uh-huh. You sell penthouses?"

"Sometimes, but really we do every kind of properties."

"And you," Tolik broke in, "what are you doing in New York?"

"We here to learn good English."

"Ah." Tolik and Gena knew their luck.

*"Chto pyem?"*[99] Gena put down the gauntlet.

"Cosmopolitan."

"Two Cosmos. Stoli Raspberry for me. Tolik, for you…?"

"Hennessy, please. VS."

Gena then knew, Tolik had raised the stakes.

"Yeah, start a tab." Gena plunked down his Amex Gold.

---

99 What are we drinking?

They toasted to their meeting and drank down. The smile returned to nest on Tolik. He was *baaack*. After the first two drinks, they were old friends. Tolik requested transfer to a table. After five minutes, they could glance each other better, from all sides.

Dasha was learning marketing in school and wanted badly to move here and get a job, enjoy New York. This city was so full of life! *You bet, for sure, you silly kid,* was Tolik's napkin estimate. Good luck.

These girls were twenty-two, not more. Sveta was quite ambitious, by the look of things. She designed scarves and ties and clothing at art institute. Business was brisk, but only local there, for now. This was their 4-week summer break.

Vodka and cognac flowed. They ordered caviar and salmon, fried potatoes—snacks. Gena slowed down, but Tolik flew, unchecked. Short of a total fuckup, this was easy tail. He hadn't drunk this much in years, poor fool, just past a comfy buzz into a gentle slur.

It got on toward midnight. Girls went to do their things. Gena, still sober, gasped at bill. $250! FML. They split, redoubled focus, waiting for their turn. Dasha and Sveta came back cautious; one had talked down the other. Gena insisted they would get chauffeured. They couldn't much refuse. *Noblesse oblige.*

Tolik led Dasha buy the waist. Gena was bolder, arm on shoulder, planting kisses. The driver took the longest route imaginable. Their dorm was part of FIT. He parked. They walked the ladies to the door. Each trapped his butterfly and kissed her deeply, overeagerly. There was no invitation up for tea forthcoming. They exchanged numbers and would be in touch.

Back in the car, the boys were optimistic, if impatient. The night air calmed the sting of vanished grasp. They'd get their own. But fuck, $250 was excessive, still. Frustration was a bitch. Their expectations and their craft had long evolved since high school. Home turf advantage had its perks, as well.

They turned off Brooklyn Bridge onto the BQE. The longer bridge now beckoned them, for maybe the ten-thousandth time. What a magnificent construction!

A Beamer—an MG—pulled even with them on the left. The window rolled down smoothly. A kid—18 or 20, not much older—challenged Gena. It was on.

By reflex, not to be outdone, Gena straight-floored it and they flew. The sunroof roared with whooshing air. The two weaved in and out—at 90, 100, then 110—with nasty, reckless, purposeful precision. This kid—probably Syrian, from Ocean Parkway—was quite good. Gena was laser-focused. A slow poke clogged the leftmost lane. A tiny window opened in the right lane and he squeezed his way, threading the needle. Score! They were the first under the bridge. *Take that, you fucking losers! M6, my ass. Let's trade! I'll show you how to drive. Dumb kids.*

Tolik rolled down his window. The water shimmered in the dark. The night was crisp. Ahead, the projects—they were always there. He'd graduated them, at least. One day, he'd look back from his own M6. The future promised great success, endless supply of riches, bitches. Not so much to ask.

# 2

# Vlad

The worst was over, he decided. Striding out through the doors of 60 Lafayette—Family Court—Vlad feigned a smile. Joe Sherman, his smooth-talking asshole lawyer chatted up a colleague, just outside. He headed west to Franklin Street. Bled dry by Dina and *her* lawyers, then by Joe, by movers, his new landlord, every sundry fucker, he charged into the freezing wind with brazen, open-mouthed relief. To hell with all the vipers from his life. At least, he got his visitation rights with Lyova—his little man, his mini-me, for every other weekend. With his late nights billed full, there was no sense in custody, regardless.

G-d, how he just wanted just to start his life again! Nine months of unadulterated hell, divorce. He had tiptoed around the minefield for too long. He could remember barely when they were in love. The nagging and abuse, recriminations, all had choked the last of their affection, long ago. She snapped about "the bitch at work," his hours and responsibilities. Vacations to Dominican, the endless fancy clothing—nothing was quite good enough for her. He should've listened; Mom was right. *That was too harsh.*

The love was real until some point. Lyova had been an accident, revealed when they had started fighting over stupid things—the better coffee press to buy, paint color for the walls. Why was he so worked up back then about such things? A newly married idiot.

He sighed. How could he fail to see all that was "obvious," supposedly? Was he not always the farsighted and pragmatic one of all his friends? Everything else in life, he'd done quite well and brilliantly, so far. This was a blight the size of Texas, this whole story. The only good thing, he was free to move on with his life.

Vlad hurried down the stairs to catch the 1. His car was mostly empty. He sat, exhaling with the force of a balloon, deflated. His hands consoled the yawning physiognomy and cupped his forehead, bulging. What a wretch. The train dragged forward, creaking, wheezing on without conviction. Toward Times Square, his appetite revived. Pretty brunette walked in, anchoring in front of him. Vlad stood instinctively and offered her the seat. She smiled and sat, a rare exemption from the kneejerk feminist refusal. A bookworm with her tote from Viking Press, her Warby Parkers and a Kindle. *Cute.* One detail warmed her quickly to his liking—hair. Dinka—before her, Luba—had the same—wavy, dark brown, a gloried treasure spilling onto shoulders. It was his thing; branded for life.

Reluctantly, he stepped out at 110. The chick made eyes at him. *Those bookish Arts & Science girls*, he thought, just waiting to be turned from feminism to quaking common sense. This nest deserved a proper look, once things calmed down. Shame he was moving out so soon. He'd miss the vibe—whatever vibe one feels at 10 at night after 14 or 15-hour days, on weekends with a wife and kid. Turns out he'd missed the scenery. Damned shame. These co-eds were spectacular.

Vlad greeted Marcos—doorman—and went up. He shed his shoes and sprawled out on the bed. Freedom or something like it—maybe piece of mind. He closed his eyes, inhaling with exaggerated force. Returning CO2, he looked up and was blank. No shitty obligations, schedule bombs, annoying girlfriends staying over, none of that. He could eat all the ice cream, white rice, deep-fried shit he wanted. No more tyranny! Well, maybe not. He had to stay in shape for all those sexy JDates and the random hookups. This time, he wouldn't waste himself on Ivy Leaguer girls—especially not other lawyers, G-d forbid. He'd had enough of mental masturbation, overthinking and the cleverness. Enjoyment by both parties and transactional efficiency, was all. Young was unquestionably better, freshness the key. His 35 wasn't exactly ancient, but he'd aged. His hairline was retreating surreptitiously, his abs in need of work. At least he had his height and silver tongue, dancing at beckon call of an obliterating mind, clever to the point of sinister intent. His clients and the partners knew it; he was next in line.

G-d, what a thrill to be alone and un-entangled! He could pinch himself. At last, he'd get to do the trips he'd long forsaken as impossible—Ibiza, Ios and then Goa, Phuket, Bali and New Zealand. *Yesss!*

His bliss felt almost shameful. There was Lyova. Hm, yes,

his Little Man. What a damned shame—he, too, would have to deal with all the awful shit of divorced parents. At least his father would be close and do his part. There would be no repeat of Edouard's mistake.

But had he not, in fact, precisely done just that? Had he not run from Dina because he was "done" with her? *Oh please, enough with Jewish guilt.* She slandered him like hopeless excrement in court, destroyed his reputation with their friends, clawed back well beyond half, then took his son. He was a squatter now, effectively—the condo would be sold, the profits split. What an inglorious defenestration. *Well, glad to know you too, bitch*!

Vlad felt a creeping heartburn. *Time to eat.* He slowly, lazily rolled out of bed and sorted through the pile of menus on the counter. Italian, Thai, Chinese. Yekh. Sushi! He dialed and ordered—Rainbow roll with edamame, special sauce and beer. If freedom, then at least in full.

He pulled out Haagen-Dazs, plopped down before the big screen and flipped through the channels. Oh, the Kardashians, The Bachelorette, Myth Busters, QVC, replays of CSI and Law and Order. Nothing satisfied. He must've missed out on at least ten years of TV shows, G-d-knows-what-priceless references from pop culture. What a boor! He wondered whether *Young and Restless* and *General Hospital* were on. He'd snuck in episodes in high school once, G-d help him, twenty years ago! Where had his endless youth just vanished? Life was cruel.

Well, he'd catch up and then some now. Time was his again. ESPN came on. Here was LeBron on breakaway to dunk, Miguel Cabrera swatting at a pitch—homerun!, Rafa returning vs. Djokovic, a NASCAR driver—Jimmie Johnson—crossing first. G-d damn it, he would dominate, as well! *Just have to get your life in order, fool!*

Wow, this was how they got subscriptions. He snapped out of it. *You sorry bastard, look at you. What kind of shmuck is gonna get a girl by sitting on his ass and eating ice cream? What is wrong with you?*

His usual resolve was failing him. Divorce was one thing, but his work had lost its thrill. Yes, he had turned a corner with his lateral move to Weil. Just as he'd wanted, he was pushed right to the front of cases, right to court. He supervised a raft of third and fourth-years, worked on Lehman, AMR, Blockbuster, all the cream. But something snapped these past few months. No longer was he thrilled to lead the charge. The Chase was soured by layoffs, grumbling partners, all the petty gossip. He was in favor and his instincts were as sharp as ever, but for what grand purpose? Short of a partnership, what had he failed to do? Not much, except or please his mother, bed Kate Upton and become a billionaire. He'd always had the urge to teach, but never time. He could finagle an instructorship at NYU, his alma mater. Sure, why not?

What was it that he really wanted from his life? To travel and enjoy? Create? No really, he was not the type; Marik had gotten all the genes for that. He liked to write, as well, but academic articles, not more. Some would suggest he go find Moses, like his cousin Boris, but no thanks. He was a man with certain tastes and views, not open to wholesale makeover à la Hari Krishna.

Perhaps this was just wishful thinking, all of it. His leave was over in 2 weeks. This morning's judgment had quite frankly killed illusions of an early exit or a year to travel, like the burned-out crowd. He had to work, make buck, pay off the mortgage—solely in his name—then make do with diminished means. He'd have to make a budget for the first time in eight years, buy his own groceries—alright, then Fresh Direct. He couldn't cook to save his life, but take-out was a fiscal black hole and a drag.

*Was there a way to have Mom cook his meals*, he wondered, *without moving in*? Pity and sympathy were strong, but this was shameless. *Maybe not…* He really asked for an endurance test. She'd have him ship-shape in no time. G-d, please have mercy on his soul—she *would.*

How could he—Vlad Gorelick, fearsome litigator, prodigy, the Great White Hope himself, be helpless to the point of desperation—Mother's care? The cord would sprout again, like magic, he well knew. He'd limit damage to 3 weeks or 4, at most, while this place sold. Worse things in life than home-cooked food—the best!—but no free lunch. He'd have to listen to life's wisdom pouring forth, unfiltered, day and night. And best of all, he'd find himself surrounded by old Brighton, Boulevard of Crippled Dreams. G-d help him, what a fall from grace. Imagine running into cousin Tolik on the Boardwalk or at Golden Key. "What a surprise! Vova, my cousin! What brings you to our charming ghetto? Miss the good times, eh?" *G-d, what a lowlife.* But what choice?

He needed to save money and that's that. The bitch he'd married had no mercy, plain and simple. *Moving on.* Vlad ruminated, head in hands. He'd stepped into a big one. No returns.

The doorbell rang. He shook himself upright and rushed to get his food. The Chinese man delivering was too familiar for his taste. "Mista Go-re-liik, here your order."

"Thank you, here's your tip." To cut things short, he gave a fiver with a wooden smile. The man was grateful, drawing quickly off.

Vlad ripped the stapled package open and dug in. Decorum, etiquette, to hell. No one was watching. It was gooood to eat. He flushed down his Hitachino—these guys knew beer—and sat back to digest. A spasm of gastric reflex brought controlled disgust. Sushi on Mondays…SHIT. Vlad felt a sudden urge to leave the premises. He dressed in haste and grabbed the keys and wallet, locked the door and ran. Staying much longer in this place would ruin him.

Outside, the wind reminded him; winter held court. Down and away from here! Students and bums, the local ghetto characters now rushed him from all sides. What did these people <u>do</u> all day, he wondered—sit on stoops? The women worked, the men just hustled? Effing awesome.

A big, black guy blindsided him, yelling out, "Yo, white boy, watch it. You just broke my glasses. You owe me fifty bucks." He held out his large palm and flicked his fingers unequivocally.

Vlad heard of this maneuver many times, but never from

experience. The guy was really rather large and didn't show the chink in armor of a mama's fool. Vlad tried the pass, but flanking a refrigerator wasn't easy. The big boy grabbed him by the coat, returning merchandise. "You heard me, asshole. Break my glasses, pay me fifty bucks."

"Don't touch me. I will *sue* your ass."

"Go 'head, white boy. Sue me for all I got. That ain't too much."

Vlad couldn't drop his jacket and run off—no way. He could just elbow him, right in solar plexus and take off, but that would cause a scene. Maybe his buddies would catch up and beat him; better not.

"I'll give you twenty bucks. That is my final offer."

"Forty, you're free."

"Fuck you. Those glasses are pure trash."

"What did you say to me?"

He lifted Vlad up by the collar, eyes bloodshot. His other first was raised, right by his sorry victim's head. *Not worth it, really. Fuck a duck.*

"Ok, just put me down. I'll give you forty."

Vlad looked around for officers, as best he could. Why is it, they were always there and *not* right now, precisely at this moment? Why did nobody stop, these prissy undergrads, or anybody else? Was it not obvious, scenario? Just effing unbelievable. New York, 2013, and *this*!

"Here." Vlad shoved it and took off. "Go choke on it, you worthless shit," he whispered under breath.

Had that just really happened? How surreal. The shock transcended even shame. He raged beyond humiliation at the cosmic scheme. What he done to merit this? He turned off Broadway, toward Amsterdam. Vlad sat down on a stoop, drew long, deep breaths—in, out, in, out—and slowly calmed. The anger wasn't worth the twenty—fuck it, forty—bucks. He wasn't hurt. The pride was tarnished slightly, but in isolation. What did he care about some ghetto asshole? He could have had him with an elbow or a punch. Ah, screw it. Just move on.

He stood and stretched his shoulders, arms, then calves. Vlad snarled and punched the air. How silly, but the wound remained. This sort of shit had happened time and time again in high school but at 35? Vlad grasped his forehead, wiping eyes.

He needed to get out of here, to clear his head. Too many kicks and slaps upside the head these last few months. Enough. He whipped his phone out, ordering a rental car. How useful—a nice Prius sitting just five blocks away. He popped into Whole Foods to grab some water for the road. Vlad couldn't pass up the baked goods entirely—no more nagging, thank you. He grabbed a couple cookies, with a lusty eye.

Standing in line, he eyed the women all around him, gritting teeth. The yoga pants—Good Lord!—all of them, fit as hell. Their gorgeous curves were gleaming in every direction. Yelp! Control yourself, unscrupulous sex addict, horny Jew!

He paid, admiring one last time. *Have a nice day*, indeed. Back up the ramp, toward his Gore mobile. Where was he going, actually? Far off this cursed island. To AC? To Philly or DC? Too far without a plan. For sure not the Five Boroughs or the Catskills… Wait. There was a spot he'd been to as a kid that once, a beach somewhere on Rockaways. Fort *something*, Jacob *something*. He researched. Fort Tilden, Jacob Riis, that's right.

The parking valet brought around the car. Vlad plugged in his iPhone and cranked up Clapton, revving out. Not quite a Chevy to the levy, but not bad. The first riffs of *Cocaine* accompanied him east. The dude was <u>sick</u>. What happened to his own guitar, he wondered.

He had a lot of work to get his mojo back, full speed. The white stuff might be fun to try… Too late. He was too old, self-conscious Mama's boy. He'd have to ask around to smoke some good stuff. It had been too long. G-d, what a shitty rebel. Useless.

*She don't lie. She don't lie, she don't lie; Cocaine.*

Down FDR, he found the sweet spot, launching Derek Trucks. This was road music, meant to be. Just as he turned off onto BQE, his reward arrived. He belted out the words. *But mama, ain't you gonna/Miss your best friend now?/Gonna have to find yourself/Another best friend, somehow./Now don't you try and move me./You're just gonna lose./There's a crash on the levee/And mama, you've been refused./Well, it's sugar for sugar/Salt for salt/If you go down in the flood/It's gonna be your own fault./Oh mama, ain't you gonna/Miss your best friend now?/Gonna have to find yourself/A new best friend, somehow./Well, that high tide's risin'/Mama, don't you let me down/Pack up your suitcase/Mama, don't you make a sound./Now it's king for king/And queen for queen./Gonna be the meanest flood/That anybody's ever seen.*

Vlad lingered for a moment in the solo. *That's the stuff.* Under the Verrazano, like the old times. *Whoosh.* Now there was Coney Island—midgets' glory. *Greeeeat.* The ugly, Soviet-style high rises were a sore reminder. They trained their creeping presence on him, middle fingers of a filthy hand. He shuddered. Memory was steel. He sped past Ocean Avenue, then C.I.A. No sooner than he had to, thanks.

He noted that the traffic was quite light. When was the last time he was on the road at 2 PM on Monday? In Miami, maybe for her 30th? Or maybe in San Fran on Labor Day, 2008, to visit second cousin Ilya? Shit, half a decade since! But *how*?

Vlad turned off toward Rockaways. A charming little place, he thought. Water in every sense, right on the beach. Water in every pore, oh boy. He now remembered what he'd read about the miles of beach, all washed away, the houses ruined, devastation. Most likely, there would be no walk. He parked as close as gates allowed. No one around, quite eerie. Nobody on the baseball fields, nobody here patrolling, just some trucks.

He snuck inside and walked across toward the fence. There would be cop cars guarding, surely. Nope! *No Trespassing*, of course. He couldn't help himself. Looking around, he listened carefully and climbed the fence. *Was he insane?* Just as he landed on the other side, he reasoned. *Must be Feds, not state.* Devil may care.

When had he pissed on rules and spat on orders last? *Conformist*! Since hanging with the hipster druggies back in Princeton, he had given up the light. Good grades, clean nose, all work, faux play. *Abra cadabra*, fifteen years, all fearful, law-abiding servitude. Always a different pharaoh, same result.

He tiptoed down the walkway, strewn with junk, graffiti, hell-knows-what-washed-up. His ears remained alert. Vlad climbed over fresh dune and looked out on the water. Sweet! The breeze was strong today; he wouldn't stay forever. Dismissing Mama's voice—"Нельзя, продует!"[100]-Vlad sat down. The place had really lost its beach-ness, in his mind. At least, he felt removed, no buildings visible, no noise. He was alone—completely, not a soul around. Just half an hour from the source. What peace! He could be mauled or shot without a ripple here, *the end*! No one would know for days to find him, just like that. His phone had lost reception, even better. Now, he just turned it off.

Vlad listened closely to the crashing waves. It was high tide. The sky was not too merciful today, neither completely overcast, nor smiling—or in danger—just a winter sky. A couple lazy gulls were circling, landing a lazy stone's throw to his left. Conditioned bastards, they examined him. Expectant, wary, patient little beasts. What could they have from him except for bitter shooing? So much for solitude. The insolence!

Groaning, he raised himself and stood upright. Vlad yawned and stretched, remaining taut, arms up. Animal force shot

---

[100] It is forbidden! You will get a chill!

through him downward, then rebounded and escaped his gullet. The primal yawning scream resounded, chasing birds away. How good and sweet and numbing, lazy days like this. He felt 15 again—hair notwithstanding, slower, with an added pouch—but damn it, wiser, *certifiably*. In practice, actually, who knew? What bliss there was in dirty jokes and aimless rambling. Oh, let me count the thousand dumbass thrills! That was his problem—Vladimir Gorelik's—too uptight, scared, hedging for too long. Doctor's advice was calling for a jolt. More recklessness, less worry. Give me sex or death!

*Dramatic, Edouardovich. You ass. Who are you, anyway? A man defined by work? A Russian Jewish Mama's boy without a violin or doctor's license? How repressed.* According to the therapist, quite so. Why had he gone, at all? To please the wife, oh yes. The wife and therapist had both forgotten to unclog, Dina to flush. New page.

Young man of contradictions and complexities! Not anymore, perhaps. The largely self-inflicted struggles of his twenties had long faded into anecdotes. Lyova was very young, still, for these bardly tales, and women Vlad did chase would listen, but not care. But really, these JDates were humorless. Who could resist his raunchy run-ins down in 'Nawlins? Who would poo-poo trespassing Texas at the State House, near-death on the Golden Gate? The same obnoxious bitches who would case his bank account—or ask, straight up. The rituals of dating had devolved completely to prehensile. When in Rome…

For all her warts, his Dina never was like this. Direct,

hammer to anvil, seek-no-cover—yes—but feminine and subtle in her moments, still. Vlad paused, staring ahead of him at water's edge. Regret blindsided him in one convincing, bitter blow. What had he done? How could he kill the golden goose? How could he spurn his wife like just another glove off hand? Had he not learned a thing from Daddy dearest? G-d, what a fool. Late hours and the flirting; she was right. Why must a woman "manage," always? Soviet rules had passed. She was no angel, but no scourge of manhood, either. A brilliant mother, in the classic style. Maybe he'd driven her away with his "requests," as well. What was he thinking, idiot? Suddenly, memories crawled out. Seville, May of 2005. Orange sundress, hair down, red lipstick, dark mascara; yellow in the background. She took off running and he chased her. The tiny streets between the cars, the Moorish doors. Frantic, back-alley capture, kissing, recognition. He took her there and there, still trembling, pulsing high and higher. How she came!

Vlad closed his eyes and placed himself back then and there. Could that exist again? How? Could that happen with another woman? Never, in million years. And what about the view in Mykonos? Such silent, utter peace of mind, together. *Why, why, why?*

He knew then that he'd blown it, just like that. Home late once from a happy hour, a missed call, a blow-up over kitchen paint. One after one, drops in a shallow bucket, then her patience drowned. You couldn't graft on "common sense" to woman; she shredded the male ego out of habit. Not only had he handled it, he strangely missed "the whip."

With any luck, the next one would be half as ballsy, tenth as sharp. She was impatient, Dinka, but what woman wasn't? *Dumbass.*

Too late, spilt milk, sand through the fingers, she was gone. With half his not-so-modest savings and his future earnings for another thirteen years. *Just keep it, dear. A bitter souvenir for both of us. You'll use the money better for the both of us, for Lyovkin. You always managed numbers better, anyway. You gorgeous, brilliant bitch.*

Fresh start was hardly zesty, at this rate. In fact, he was a raging mass of hormones, nonsense and delusions, it was clear. For an accomplished litigator, he was pretty useless in accounting. *Let someone else just run the numbers. Send me the report. Mom, Dina or the shrink—whoever, you decide. I'm one of X percent with this condition. Not so terrible. Be my support group. You discovered it. I can't just work on this myself! Oh well. I've got too much already on my plate. Try me again, next year.*

*Kretin! Outsourced your decency, as well. Well, there you go. Congrats.* Vlad sat down in the sand again. It yielded poorly, but he didn't mind. He closed his eyes and breathed the salty air. *Ladno, vsye viydet, kak nibud,* he thought. Mom always said. It's true. *This was a different, chosen hell. The first divorce was forced on him by circumstance, the second one imposed by law. The third attempt at bliss would yield more easily. That's it.* He did his best to mimic yogic breathing. Belly out, air in through nostrils, gut in, then breath out. He straightened up, repeating cycle, then once more.

A loud voice made him jump and hit the sand, in pain. "Hey you, get out of here!"

Vlad thoroughly freaked out. "Oh shit," he whispered.

"I should arrest you, asshole, for trespassing. You're in big trouble. This is a national park."

Involuntarily, Vlad froze and mumbled. The old trick surfaced—play the immigrant. "I sorry, vot is problem, officer? I only vok hear. It is problem?"

"Yes, a big problem, How did you get here?"

"Just vok on bitch, like zis." He pointed out along the shore. "I stay viz friends in Rock-evey. It problem, I just go. I sorry, no spik English good. I visit from my country, Russia."

"What. Is. Your. Name? Do. You. Have. ID?" The officer pronounced with painful slowness.

"ID? Like passport?"

"Yes, or driver's license."

"One second." Vlad felt his pockets frantically. "I sorry, I forgot at house. I walk and get for you." *What house*? Why was he lying? This was madness. He fucked things up completely. *Trespassing, lying to an officer.*

The latter scrounged his face and looked Vlad up and down. Luckily, he had put on something half-presentable.

"Ok Sir, come with me." They walked in silence for eternal minutes on the ruined beach. Vlad's heart was flitting like a wild bird, caged. At least six months in jail, high fine, career most likely finished. Probably disbarment. Through the ordeal, he held his piss and gripped his teeth. *Mouth shut, mouth shut.* Maybe the guy was nice. Maybe this was for show. If he had backup, then they'd book him. *G-d, save me, let me out of this alive, without arrest. Please! I'll be better, I will do Kippur!* He prayed behind his half-smile mask. *Just let me out! I'll be a better father, not touch shiksas, name it. Please, just let me go!*

The officer, annoyed and tired, unlocked the gate. "Alright, Sir. Here's the deal Normally, I'd arrest you or at least give you a ticket. I'm feeling nice today. I'll let you off with just a warning. Remember, if I see you here again, I <u>will</u> arrest you and <u>big</u> trouble. Got it?"

"Yes, officer, I un-de-stend. I very sorry. Senk you. Have nice day."

"Alright. Bye-bye." He locked the gate back up and eyed the over-grateful Russian, as he turned away. Slowly, Vlad turned and walked away, straight line, nose forward, swinging arms. He counted sixty seconds twice and turned his head just slightly back to check. The guy was gone. He broke into a run, beelining for his car. A weight the size of Alcatraz had lifted from his shoulders, tensed. He beamed and giggled, grateful. The overgrown teenager took off quickly.

As he went over, back across the bridge, he swore, "G-d, thank you, you have saved me. Thank you, <u>really</u>. I'm gonna be a good boy now, date only Jewish girls. Well, I will do my best. Plus, minus." Oof, what great escape. No, never any more like this.

Vlad felt the spark of hunger in his soul again. *Yeah, that's the stuff!* Weaving through traffic, naughty boy hatched plans, even if G-d would laugh.

# 3

# Marik

Rage flickered through his pounding lids, convulsing arms and pillows over head. The cringing buzz repeated from the nightstand, an obscene barrage. A hellish sunlight hovered on his back like a slow-heating iron.

Mark cradled up inside the ditch of his disgust, refusing to surrender to the aftermath. What fucking asshole was disturbing him this early, with persistence? He felt a strong need to reach out and grab—a breast, a buttock, round and fleshy something to draw close, caress. Val was long gone. The smell of perfumed lotion lingered in the sheets. It could have roused a carcass or Bob Dole.

Resigned, he threw off the duvet, half-moaning, grumbling to sit up. The phone continued buzzing. 3 messages, 5 calls, 9 texts. To hell with all of them. Brother, sister, even Mom could wait. First, water and a Tylenol. Fuck, надо меньше пить. [101]

---

[101] Must drink less. [reference to a famous Soviet movie, where the main character drinks too much and ends up in the wrong city, wront apartment and with the wrong woman, on the night when his engagement party took place.]

The bathroom light screwed up his face. He drew back out and wiped his eyes. *Never again. Never forget.* The April Fool was 33, Jesus's age at death. He'd made it, barely just. What horror, he was far advanced. Rinsing his face, Mark now arranged his hair. Thinning brown hair, kangaroo pouch, poor posture, circles under eyes. It was a puzzle, time like this, what women found attractive in him still. His charm—the endless charm of Mark Gorelik, author, blogger, spender extraordinaire. For women, wine and song—king's ransom, please. He still had a few thousand left to live on until payday, on June 1st.

The phone rang once again. No fooling Mom.

"Alyo? Privet, Mom. How are things?"

"Moy Marik, Happy Birthday! Congratulate you, wish you everything to turn out. Book, job, with Valya. *Sinok*, it's time to marry, family to start. This is your year. I pray for you each day."

Mark rolled his eyes.

"Spasibo, Mom. Which year already, 'it is time?' Not everything's so simple, but please G-d."

"You sleep late again? Вставай, вставай, дружок, с постели на горшок!" [102]

"Okh, Mamonka. You're great. A moment's peace is not allotted on this earth (*Pokoya netu na zemlye.*) Day of my birth, of all! So I slept late, and what?"

---

102 Get up, get up, my little friend, from the bed to the chamberpot. [from a Russian ditty used to wake up children]

"Ранняя пташка получает червя." [103]

"Mom, leave it."

"Fine, Marik. Won't bother you. *Davai, davai.* I kiss you. Happy Birthday!"

"*Davai, spasibo Mom.* By you, everything's fine?"

"All's fine. As usual."

"Nu, good, ok. Mom, off I go."

"Wait, wait. Forgot to ask. How was the shindig? Celebrated well?"

"First-rate. Everyone came Zhenya and Anya, Sasha, Lera, Tom, the twins, evern Moshe came from Boston. It was a riot. Здорово. [104] Kiddos were left at home, we sang the potpourri, played the guitar. Like in the good old times."

"Happy to hear. Kiddos…"

"'*…for self, it's time. Grandkids, I want.*' We're done. I run, I run."

"*Begi, malish.* I kiss you."

"*Poka.*"

"*Poka, poka.*"

He shook his head. Relentless, Mom. G-d bless her. But how much could be take? 32, what's the rush? Now 33.

---

103 The early bird gets the worm.

104 Awesome.

Men ripened slowly and aged well. His type, especially—the clever humanist. Steel balls and silver tongue on stilts. Women clung on to each one of the three, straight to his bed of roses, when convinced. Val was a good kid, sharp, but young. A tigress in the sack. On good days, he felt 23 with her; on others, Humbert Humbert. How long he'd feed her Great Man complex was unclear. More likely, she would leave, like all the others had, tired of his outbursts and self-loathing between feasts and monologues. His early triumphs—Granta, Kenyon and Paris Review—were ancient history by now. The deadline for his novel was approaching fast. Scribner and agent Andrew hounded him for chapters now. His ink had trickled to a stop, the brilliance of Part I subverted by the woman and an odd malaise.

It all began the night they met at Zhenya's party, when she hooked him. The wench had thrashed his nemesis, Greg Shpilkin.

"That no-good, pandering self-hater. What a waste!"

*Yes please, I'll have another*, he remembered thinking.

"He *is* quite good at travel writing," he dead-panned.

"Ha! With an expense account, I'd give them pearls too, each time. I'd name my first child, Condé Nast."

Laughs all around. Shpilkin, the bastard child, had managed an appointment—NYU, a regular New Yorker gig, a three-book deal and status as de facto face of Russian Jewish letters. Travesty!

Why did he have to spoil his mood? It was *his* day, Dinner at Balthasar tonight, a reading at Anna's Salon, celebratory, non-cerebral sex. He'd made a clean break and was keen not to return. The dark shit he had waded through for years was past. Misery's prose was company enough. And yet, the therapists and meds had failed to chase the tinge of doubt that lingered in the sheen of smiles, the cheers and laughter on a sunny day, the novelty of gadgets and new faces. The old miasma of reflexive criticism, recast as helpful impulse, carried on. But what else did he know? If he could not perfect it, it was flawed for good. Without a buffer—woman—he would self-digest, reverting to a primal state of frightful OCD and blame and wasted time. Whole carcasses of days washed up, at will, in dregs of memory.

Mark shuddered, reaching for his first edition *Buddenbrooks.* He scrambled to his safe zone—writing desk and chair—and turned on Bach's Double Concerto. Perlman and Zuckerman. Deep breath. His eyes closed on the imitation world. Red velvet curtains drew to shield the chamber orchestra from noise. The stream began.

Charles—protagonist—would madly fall in love with his coworker Sara, take her for a weekend in the Berkshires. She would not speak much—mostly listen—but contribute just the word or phrase to finish every sentence. Her deep, green Jewish eyes were feeding him the secrets of the universe across the dinner table. The future of their life together spread out through a gorgeous landscape, adventures in creation of new worlds—the corporal, essential drawn from her, his words illuminated grandly, of their own accord, in a medieval manuscript containing ancient truths. Their partnership—a union iterated from a prior life—would be the wellspring of great things.

In Part 2, they would marry. He would write. She'd tend to house; he'd contemplate. She'd look on in her timeless beauty, effortless. In Part 3, he would undertake his magnum opus. It was a piece of staggering complexity and craft that was well-liked by all, triumphant in its neo-modernism. The trance expired with crescendo. Mark fumbled with the pen and notebook to record the flow. One didn't question when it came. The secret of the gift was this—condition-setting, prayer, never trapping butterflies.

The drug was working. He got up, refreshed. As always, he was running late for lunch, this time Gramercy Tavern and with Andrew. He showered with a put-on zeal, brushing his teeth, then shaving on the fly. He sprayed his good cologne, old Zegna Z, and quickly dressed. Mark jumped inside a cab.

Andrew was waiting at a table in the back. His look of "friendly shark" belied a backlog of unpleasant news. Mark braced himself.

"Hello there, birthday boy! Sit down, what will you have to drink?"

"Andrew! I'm good. A few too many just last night."

"Come on, old man. Aren't you Russian, after all?"

Statements like this had always grated Mark to point of wanting to switch agents, time to time.

"Yes, sure, but Russians all die early thanks to booze. Trust me, I would. Just not today." He sat. "How's business?"

"Business is pleasure, through and through, my friend. No three-martini lunches lately, but we can't complain."

"Too much."

"Mark, I won't lie. Steinberg is giving me a lot of shit because of you. You have Part II for me? You promised it 3 weeks ago, remember?"

"Not with me, but it's close to done."

"Again, it's 'close to done?' Come on, Mark, cut the crap. What is the problem now? You out of money? Woman trouble? Talk to me. I need you to deliver, man."

The lump of shit just barely cleared his throat. His leash was short already. This was bad.

"Look, it's been hard. I've hit a dry spell lately—with my writing."

"Why don't you tell me, Mark? I'm on your side, remember? You getting laid?"

Mark squinted with a held disgust. This frat-boy, buddy-buddy manner crossed the line.

"Don't be concerned. I'm fine, well-rested, busy. Just need a spark. It happens, writer's block."

"Not on my watch. We've got 5 months exactly to give them a book. You've barely done Part I and there are two to go. Figure it out. You have a week. I need Part II or Steinberg will take us to court. Don't take him for a fucking fool. Me neither, for that matter, Mark. I'm tired of the excuses. I run a business, not Good Will."

"Alright, I hear you loud and clear. You'll have Part II this week. No more excuses. You are right. I'll get my act together."

"I know you will. Just had to make my point. Chill out, I told you, lunch on me. I'll ask again, what will you have to drink?"

"A sidecar. Thanks."

Slowly, his rage subsided under forced reciprocation, smiles, backslapping and false laughter. How thoroughly he would've told him off… Free lunch! If book contracts were easy come, Goodbye!

The sidecar was quite good and strong. Contempt melted away, and went. Together with duck liver moose and then the arctic char came Nero d'Avola and Riesling. Mark had decided mid-way through the meal, he'd buckle down, but first, get his 15% worth from his frenemy.

The chocolate pudding with the salted caramel and toffee popcorn was a revelation. A Tawny Port was fitting as an end note. Maybe this Andrew wasn't bad. Things would work out. They parted ways.

Clouded with leering judgment, Mark took Broadway down into Union Square. Even his whiskeyed conscience could not well prevent unease from dampening his mood. He had a week to do two months of work, blank cartridge trumping the blank slate. Whom was he kidding, he was screwed. Worse, writing was impossible today. Between the public dress-down and the birthday thrill, his mind was over-stretched and firing well beyond his writer's pale. *How was it that his broken record didn't fail to play after a threat?* He had to calm his nerves.

He picked up an espresso to revive. Sitting in Union Square, he drank the shot with feigned relief. The sun was only tentative. He shivered from the breeze. The students and the motley loiterers annoyed him.

Vova and Alla—*serious* adults—were working now, this moment, making buck. He was, at 33, freelancing still, treating advances as play money. His brother and his sister, both, were sober family folk, advanced in asset acquisition, with small kids in tow. And he, the youngest—"Little Shit"—was unattached, subletting, living check to check. His freedom was ephemeral, if sweet. No licking ass, no 9-to-5, no ladders and no snakes for him. His impulsivity and striving were the consolation prize. He hungered always for new nuggets, hidden ironies, minutiae, turns of phrase. His memory was phenomenal, thank G-d.

At least he was ahead in life of cousin Tolik. That one had never even finished college, bummed on Brighton, did some shady things. Once Mark had heard, he programmed porn sites, dabbling in scams. He was *this* close to jail, if not for Vovka. What a waste. Nor had he gone in search or found himself religious without hope. That was all Boris—"Boruch"—Tolik's brother. One screwy family, Aunt Ira's.

How cruel was time. Twenty-five years ago, they came,

both families to New York. The cousins played together all the time. Mom moved them out of Brighton quickly, to a better life. Sasha divorced and struggled, never got his footing. The boys were with their mother. Both were smart. When she remarried, Tolik went haywire. Already 17, he up, moved out, made money, fucked around, big shot. How sad. Boris, the gentle soul, put up—stepfather was the beating type—but left the house, then off to college, never coming back. Better religion than "big turd, small puddle," that's for sure.

Big sister Alka-Galka rang.

"Hey, little brother. Happy Birthday! 33! You're getting really old. Not funny anymore. Go make some babies, make some money. It is time."

As always, her contempt was dipped in "humor." What she begrudged him was unclear.

"Thanks, Sis. How are my boys? Give them a kiss for Uncle Marik. How are things?"

"Just fine. They miss you. You should come sometime." The guilt trip—she could not resist.

"Invite me, then I'll come," he let.

"Come anytime. Just call ahead."

"Maybe I will. Thanks for the call. Listen, I have to run."

"Alright, enjoy. Don't be a stranger. Bring Valya with you. We'd love to meet her, *all* of us."

"Uh-huh. *Davai*, privet to Ari and the little ones."

"*Poka*."

Her icy undertone still irked him after all these years. She was the oldest, yes, and always first, accomplished beyond words, well set in life. What did she want from him? Why did he feel shit splattered on each time? *Adult voice in the room, "tough love," my ass,* he thought. She hated him for some odd reason, he could feel. Jealous of what exactly, poverty and meds? The amniotic, all-engulfing mother's love that stuck to him? Bipolar visions where he killed himself, just after he invented a new novel form? How byzantine, yet terse, female psychology. Hysterics, clinginess, and envy, world-historic! May G-d be with her.

He'd had enough. Mark had to move, chase off the rust. Instinctively, he walked toward his SoHo office, a co-working space. Two hours to kill, it would be just enough. Jazzed up, he turned the corner to go south. On University, he felt a stream approaching him. A fine, long-haired brunette—Italian, likely—then a buxom redhead strutted. Two olive-skinned Israeli girls passed by, acknowledging his gaze. They were all twenty, still in college, fresh, unspoiled. G-d help him, he was energized. Old dirty bastard had it in him, still. How could he marry and commit? His love for women was a founding myth, the simple syrup of enjoyment, vigor of his word. Life was good.

Mark took the requisite detour. Wash Square, his favorite repository, was a nest! What a mistake, college away from here. Alas. Was is just him or were the girls all smiling at him as they passed? Fate was a tease.

He sat a ways off from the fountain to assess. Was this the year when women would begin to fall like giddy birds into his willing lap? *Shit*, 33. His father was a father twice, by then! Was he like this, as well, a bearded adolescent—at *his* 33? A handsome man, that cheating bastard, but a first rate bard. Had he been scared, dried out of verse, afraid of death by moral duty? Easy to judge—*he* always had!—but harder much, to face the music. *Father...*

Mark hated all this taking stock. It was a petty, thankless, quite unnerving exercise, forced on oneself by women, normally. Past 30, birthdays lost their silver lining in this way. The only hope was just to plow ahead and write like hell, avoid submission to the feminine *moustique*, achieve a status and then speak of marriage, maybe. He always thought that Vovka had rushed into things, and look what happened. Mdaaaam. Some sage advice was overdue. If not for worthless Father who abandoned them, he would have been less skeptical of surrogates—his uncle, passing father figures and professors, too.

The old repentant fool had surfaced lately on his sickbed—but it was too late. What peace was to be made? 25 years! Into the ether, poof! There were half-brothers—2—both younger, early 20s. It was bewildering to think, a parallel reality of blood and flesh in Moscow. Edouard Yablonskiy had long made his choice. What business did he have intruding in their lives, a ghost who stood tall in their childhood photos with assured cleft chin, too-clever eyes, dashing and dark, a fraud.

*Otets* was dying. Why else would he call? In his offended

crouch, Mark failed to see the obvious. Of all of them, he was the most Yablonskiy, with his fleshy nose below the trademark widow's peak and then, of course, the chin. The gene for thick black hair had skipped him—his was reddish-brown. His gift for language was the clearest sign, Mom said. The elder often would compose a ditty on the spot at parties, play it on guitar right then and there. He was well known at *MGU* and played on stage, from time to time. Nikitini were friends and Okudjava came to hear him once.

*Folklore redeemed the human tragedy of family*, Mark thought, *but to what end*? Nobody needed Edouard, in truth. They were all grown, two with their own kids, pushing 40. He—Mark—remained the only one with vested interest in knowing, but then what? He needed it like plague or wrongful amputation, "reconciliation."

The bitterness and hurt resurfaced briefly like a fetid turd, but didn't linger. Edouard's bad state and age had humanized him suddenly. His voice had been so strangely frail, contrite, yet full of music, even *nostalgie*. Pity was not familiar for *this* man. Another day, perhaps, it might bear fruit.

Mark stretched his limbs and sauntered on. He sat down at his desk, took out his black Moleskine and lucky Bic and plugged in favorite Scarlatti. *Sonata in E Major* was a trigger piece. The playful counterpoint pushed out the base thoughts of denial, delay, protest and urge. He wrote.

The plot was coalescing neatly for Part 2. Importantly, the tap was on and flowed. Phrase after phrase, one flourish, then another, he immersed himself. Inside the throne room where he hadn't dwelt in weeks, not hipster geeks, nor Rachel, friendly manager onsite, could tempt derision or his lust. His lungs filled hungrily anew. The wherewithal had dropped from heaven as a gift. Mark swooped and parried in the clouds, a battered bird nursed back to health. The hour passed without a notice, in the conscious stream. Repeated trembling in his pocket went unanswered. Suddenly, the music ceased. Val had enough of texting with a silent wall.

"Where are you, babe? You're late. Your friends are here. We're waiting."

"Shit, sorry, I was writing, babe. And really well, too, you'll be proud. I'll be there right away. I'm only two blocks down."

"You better. We're all hungry. Come!"

Mark ground his teeth, resentful. He'd really rather keep on with it 'til exhaustion, frankly. Well, damn it, there was no way out. Resigned, he pounded on the desk and put away the notebook, up and left.

He kissed Val and then hugged his college buddy, Gabe. The wife, Loreen, was visibly with child. Mark cocked his head and upped his brows.

"That's right, you're gonna be an uncle, you old fart!"

"Quite happily, but Gabe—a father?! Oy. You guys! Loreen, you're looking great. My powers of intuition tell me… it's a boy."

"How do you know?" Gabe knew this shtick.

"The belly, dear. It's all about the shape. Plus, boys mean good complexion."

"Really?! Never heard of this."

Gabe qualified, "A Russian old-wives' tale."

"Don't knock the wisdom, man. It has its charms."

"Speaking of wisdom, how's your book?"

"Coming along. Just had lunch with my agent earlier. Choice species, let me tell you. He wants two months of work from me, next week."

Val saw an opening. "So, good! You'll give him what he wants."

Mark shot a flaming look her way. She smiled, entirely undeterred.

"Mark had a breakthrough just this afternoon. The book will be a huge success, you'll see."

"Here's my new agent, guys!" They laughed.

*Stands by her man*, thought Mark. He kissed her on the cheek.

"Heeey, look who's here! Lana and Garik! Guys, what a surprise! I didn't know you were in town! Wait, flowers, really? *That's* a first. You are too much. My goodness! Thank you! *And* a book? Nu, guys. You're crazy. Sit!"

"Look now or later?"

"Now!" ordered Lana and her Garik, in one voice.

Marik was touched profoundly and tore in.

"Oooh! Look, my favorite Brodsky and… what is this?"

Val, read for him. "Called 'I Will Teach You To Be Rich.' *That* wouldn't hurt." She winked at Lana and Loreen.

Gary stepped in to clarify. "Look, Marik, we all know you're brilliant as a writer, but the finance part could use some work. We love you and we know you'll put that Shpilkin in his place. *Davai*, let's go. This is your year."

*Some backhand compliment*, Mark thought, but they meant well.

"Gee, thanks guys, that's quite thoughtful of ya. I'll definitely put it to good use," he lied.

"If not—more likely, I will likely use it well." Val was asserting some unknown new right today. Mark noted, it would be 12 months next week—their anniversary. Still, it was wrong to gang up on the birthday boy. A low blow, from a venture capitalist—Gary; punishable sin from Val.

The waitress took their orders. Val pushed his favorites—foie gras and Taittinger Cuvée Prestige. It was a weakness; Mark acceded. They toasted their dear Marik to the gills, his eccentricity and humor and imagination, holy treasures. The friends agreed, he was a fragile soul, a buoyant intellect, a loyal friend—too gullible at times, lost in the world-historical and grand ideas, a bit not of this world, but what a guy!

Mark listened, smiling, filled with cringing dread. He was not one for compliments, especially in his presence. And yet, the bubbly—heaven-sent—had layered nicely with the liver's butter, loosening The Grouch. He hardly cared to deprecate himself, just to enjoy.

The main course came. Duck Confit, paired superbly with St. Emilion. Ripe with the weight of Gabe's ascent two steps ahead in life, Mark felt the duty tug, to toast.

"Hear, hear. In light of Gabe's impending fatherhood, I want to wish for all of us that, well… the coming generation will be better than is ours. I'm really happy for you guys. Same for *you* two. L'Chaim!"

"Hey Marik, soon by *you*!" Gabe winked.

"Indeed! Here, hear! Get busy, Mark!" Gary piled on. Mark raised his hand, as if to swat, but even so, half-heartedly. Val gave a look that stung right through veneer of silence.

*She must be punished*, Mark resolved.

"Ease up, amigos. My intentions are sincere."

His declaration was a shock to him, as much as to the gathered. Had he just made the leap like some romantic fool? The footing felt much surer, but my G-d! The wine was talking or uncovered decency?

Mark sat up tall and bore his cross with honor.

"Val, thank you, you're the best. A toast to Val, who somehow manages to deal with me. A hard case, we all know. I love you, babe, you're great. To you!"

They were all stunned.

"Now for the camera, once more!" Gabe was an ass, but lovable. Val softened up and smiled. The cloud of sarcasm lifted from her brow. The friends took note and changed their tune. Lana could not resist.

"Nu guys, you're great together. Here's to you! За Марка и за Валю!" [105] She barely could restrain a наконец.[106]

Mark drank. Loosened, he tapped the opening bars of Schumann's A Minor Concerto. What was the matter with him? Was he nuts? This morning, she was just his bedmate, and now *this*? No, it was justified. She planned this and last night's, as well. She cleaned his place and cooked quite well. They'd talked about the move-in earlier that week. His friends were all big fans.

And yet, he was afraid. It was a trap. His writing would descend to mediocrity. He'd lost his edge, his cultivated self. *What* edge? His sorry ass was shooting blanks already for how long? She was a gem.

Just then and there, he saw with perfect clarity, he'd never have another woman close to this. What was he but a struggling writer, way behind in life, just lovable and sharp enough to interest her and trap her in his silvery web of words? And now he would abandon her for some abstract idea? No way. Too many of the writers' set he knew had flushed their trump card once too often, in their hot pursuit. Plus, Mom was right—without a word, as usual—from afar. Her water torture of folk wisdom had prevailed.

---

105 Toast to Marik and Valya.

106 At last.

Mark lingered on his Val and kissed her cheek with oomph. He whispered, "Thank you, babe, You've really made an awesome birthday for me. I'll thank you properly tonight." He winked.

Val smiled. "Alright. Well, since you've been a good boy, you can have your gift."

She handed him an oblong box. He held it, puzzled, studying, then tore in. A Montblanc fountain pen! He laughed involuntarily. His childhood dream from age thirteen. Why had he wanted it so much? To write great poetry, while seated in his *kabinet* of books? Meanwhile, his Bics had served him splendidly throughout.

"You are amazing, Val. How did you know? I always wanted one when I was little. Wow."

"You'll write long thank you notes to fans after you're published, babe. Enjoy it in good health."

"Ты просто лапочка. Спасибо! Как приятно." [107] He kissed her mightily, to cheers.

"Alright, you lovebirds. Now, *our* gift." Gabe walked around the corner and retrieved a heavy bag. "Behold."

"Nespresso?! Whoa, that's nuts! You guys!"

"Big boy, you need good coffee. You'll write better."

Adulthood had arrived, with one decisive blow. Touched, Mark was short of words. Val quickly signaled for dessert.

---

107 You're just a dear. Thank you! What a pleasure.

Salon was starting in fifteen. His chocolate cake was served with candles lit. Mark wished for great success with book and Val—for her to stick around. He even got his birthday song. Garik and Gabe swooped in and split the bill. The stubborn *cause célèbre* was bested just this once.

They ran the couple blocks and sat in back, inside. The gallery was peppered with the sundry Russian artists of the moment, from the motherland. Up front, the slender, towering Anna introduced Marina Gromkina, a well-known journo-essayist from Moscow. Her work for Kommersant, the Moscow Times and glitzy Sigma magazine was edgy, but not shattering. She made a solid buck among the Global Russian set with speeches at Carnegie Fund and CFR, en editorial or two for Wall Street Journal, IHT. Her talk was on the state of Russian opposition and its chances in unseating Putin in the coming years. Sochi Olympics, Udaltsov, Navalny, then Kasparov, one big mess.

Gromkina rambled on and on forever—so it seemed. Mark, half-asleep with terrible food coma, dosed. Despite the monotone, his mind reacted like a wildfire to the name "Yablonskiy." He questioned Val if Edouard was the name. Confirmed. He sat up on fine needles, focused as a greyhound. Yablonskiy, noted physicist, was forming yet another opposition group. The fact itself of novel opposition was a scant surprise. The mention of the name was jarring, all the same. Was it imperative to feel a pride? An anger at the failure to apprise? Was that why he had called? Did Alla, Vovka know? What kind of way was this learn of Father's doings, from a journalist?

Ahead three rows, he quickly noticed a familiar balding pate. His brother? What the hell? Not in the least his scene. What was he doing here? After some girl, already out at pasture? Maybe, just maybe, he was here to wish him happy birthday, to listen to his ramblings, written down? Vova had never taken interest in his little bro's affairs, not even Val. Why now?

Marina finished up. She took two questions. Vova stood up, determined.

"What are Yablonskiy's chances, frankly, to unite the opposition? We all know he's no Sakharov and no Kasparov, either. Why do you think he bothers, even, to come forth?

Oof, he was off his rocker, Mark could tell. Edouard—*Papá*—had clearly made the rounds by telephone. He'd pissed off Vova, Level-Headed One. Well done!

"I do not know his motivations personally. Edouard is active for some years in liberal circles and has organized events, like this one, a Salon. It is a forum for economists and scientists to discuss reforms. He's not what you might call "grassroots," but charming, handsome and well-spoken. Navalny is the brash young rabble-rouser. Yablonskiy is the theorist. Nobody is expecting them to get along or lead a revolution soon. If the Olympics fail, Putin will look quite bad. This may become their opening. We'll see."

Luckily, Vova kept his mouth shut and sat down. Mark was unsettled. This was all kinds of big and sudden—and potentially a headache. Would Russian agents tail them and harass? And did they even count as family, anyway?

Yablonskiy had a second (and "real") family in Moscow. That was rough.

He couldn't help remembering the episode at Fairway two years earlier. Shopping for bread and milk, he ran broadside into Kasparov, blurting out in Russian, "Вы случайно не Каспаров?" [108]

The fearsome champion of the world was frightened like a bird and mumbled quickly a denial—senseless, awful—and took off. Would he run into his birth father in New York, as well, like this, in two years' time? Did Edouard have too much to lose by leaving Russia? He had betrayed his children once. What was a second instance to him?

Amid the clapping, Val looked over, worried. The cloud above his eyes was worrisome enough and worse yet for the coming stage time. Reluctantly, he spilled the beans on *Papochka* Yablonskiy, then his brother, right in front. Taken aback, Val searched for what this meant for them, in light of proclamations from tonight. Without realization, she tucked back her hair, lifting her blouse to hide her cleavage, straightening up.

"Alright, be calm. That's quite some news, but we'll discuss at home. Better be ready for your turn."

She took out printed pages from her purse, from Chapter 2 of his Part I, with notes typed up in margins, as he'd asked. Of course, he hadn't practiced reading much, despite her admonitions. Taking a breath, he dove right in and read, unnerved.

---

[108] Are you not Kasparov, by chance?

Anna returned to front with introduction number two, to move things on. The next contestant took the podium, one Chava Greenberg. Born in the States of Russian parents, Chava was a young 'un. Pretty and stately, she was dressed in skirt and sleeves, apparently religious too. She'd cut her chops uptown, penning a column weekly at Columbia on women's issues, with a Jewish twist. This managed to go viral, landing her in *Forward*, *Algemeiner*, *JPost*, then somehow the Times. A journo, she was also writing fiction on the side.

While Mark raced through the pages, Chava read from "Woman's Tithes," her tongue-in-cheek collection of short stories about growing up religious in a Russian household. After the second chuckle by the crowd—she'd hit a nerve—Mark lifted eyes to hear. Her writing was not feministic—overly—or peppered with neuroses, navel-gazing, as the norm. It was refreshing, thoughtful and surprising. For sure, this was the only way to get him interested at all. Upon inspection, she was quite a looker—blonde and shapely—25, at most. At minimum, he'd have to speak with her at length at one of these confabs, without the threat of jealousy from Val. She was a lettered woman, Chava, lots to say. The thought of union passed in firm succession with great clarity and stalled.

*Gorelik*! He drew back. *Focus, cabrón*! Bodega Spanish had a way with him in fevered times. Applause rang out, enthusiastic, not just for her youth. Tough act to follow, but his fight was on. A fawning geront asked technique, a softball that she parried well, with humor. A younger fart, engaged her on the role of woman in the "Orthodox Establishment," then writing as an act of protest. Mark strained his eyes to catch a glance at this pretender, voice familiar from somewhere. No, he was going crazy—was that cousin Boris? Why in G-d's name was Holy One descending here to dwell with pigs and poets, unannounced? If not for him, more likely for the girl. He was just 29, but "old" in the religious world and overdue to marry. Well, *this* was turning into one fantastic comedy of errors. These two were painted birds tonight. *Let them fly off together then*, he thought.

His turn was up. Anna gave out a trademark smile and introduced him. "Mark got his Bachelors in English Literature from Brown. Ben Zelig was his mentor at Columbia, where he received his MFA. Mark's essays and short stories have been published in *Paris Review* and *Granta* and *Kenyon Review.* He will be reading from his novel-in-progress, "Good Time Charlie." Without further ado, Mark Gorelik!"

Mark walked up to the mike. Applause went up, with unexpected cheering. He squinted, holding with appreciation. He pulled his hipster glasses out. For long as he remembered, Mark had always had a mind to demonstrate "arrival" in this way—and looked out onto audience. What friends he had! He made out Olga, Inna, Tom and Lera, Yulia. Vovka now gestured with his hand to temple. Borka waved. Val blew a kiss.

Mark sat up on the barstool, pulled the mike toward him and cleared his throat. With a peculiar strength of voice and poise, he read as if his life depended on it. (How had he managed to avoid these readings up to now?) And so, he told the story of his Charlie's accident, the flashback to his birth and weaning, mother's anxious fawning, his pursuit of Ruthie, college love.

Between the paragraphs, he paused to breathe and looked out, noting the reactions. No question, there was interest, enthusiasm. He pressed. The last two sentences, he carried off with extra flair. The corners of his mouth curled up. He knew without a doubt, he'd nailed it.

The gallery roared, taken with Mark. Solid first act. Someone in back—no way, Gary and Gabe!—was whistling lustily. *Embarrassing.* A slew of hands went up for Q&A. There was Professor Zelig gesturing with thumb, *fantastic*!

Mark called on a bright-eyed brunette. She looked like Katya, an old ex.

"What pushes you to write from one day to the next and do you ever get writer's block?"

"What pushes me? My Russian Jewish mother and my girlfriend. Who *needs* self-motivation?" *What a hoot.* "But seriously. You know this writing thing is like an itch. You scratch it, it just itches more. Leave it alone, it drives you nuts, sometimes *completely* nuts. No way to win, just keep on with it, day by day. Eventually, you get results. There's also discipline and deadlines, agents, all of that. But also, certainly, there is an urge to tell a story. It is like giving birth, in a particular male way."

He picked an older gentleman who made him think of Edouard. In broken English, he received, "Why you no write about your Russian childhood?"

Mark's fury built up instantly. He knew this school of thought too well, but from the other side, *Ugly American.* He grated teeth, preventing curse.

"You see, we've been in America for almost twenty-five years. I grew up mostly here. It's what I know the best. Of course I'm Russian by my birth, but don't consider what I write a part of 'Russian literature.'"

His gall for Shpilkin and his mid-brow handlers stayed subsumed. This was neither the time nor place.

Preventing awkward silence, Anna closed the session with a thank you and an invitation to partake and browse. After applause died, people made a beeline right for him. Just then it hit him, Mama should be here. She'd planned the trip to Italy a year ago, so nothing could be done. This was his validation with her, by the way. Real pity and a shame.

Val practically alighted in his arms. The reading really hit a nerve, he saw. She whispered in his ear, "Proud of you, babe. Let's not stay here too long. I've got a gift for you back home."

Point taken, he assured her solemnly, with winks. Vova appeared and hugged his brother with a certain desperation. Sensing a flood held back, Mark promised him they would get together in a day or two.

"Listen, I'm sorry, not tonight. Meet Val, my girlfriend. My brother, Vova."

His brother's trademark poker face was wiped, his falcon's focus vacuous and lost in thought. His posture slumped, dark circles adding misery. Where was the deal shark with the Zegna suit, impatient with the slightest inefficiency? Good G-d. Bad news.

Now Boris wandered up, his friendly grin dispersing an unease. At least he had the sense to hide his *tsitsis*[109], Mark perceived. Congratulations and good wishes flowed, an invitation—Shabbat dinner and the rest. His teacup eyes, so piercing and jade green, projected zeal. He fit the guise of prophet more than programmer, it seemed.

"Yes, yes, of course."

"I mean it, guys. We have a group of people over just like this for dinner often."

"Really?"

"Yeah! Just because I'm observant doesn't mean I'm in a synagogue all day. By the way, Mark, I think you're really talented. You know that Dedushka Aaron was writing quite a lot?"

"Had no idea. How do you know?"

"I kept his notebooks when he passed."

"Как интересно. I'll take you up on that. I want to see them." [110]

"You're welcome, any time."

---

109 Prayer shawl fringes

110 How interesting.

"So sorry, babe. This is my cousin Boris, from my father's side."

"Valya."

"Очень приятно. Come together! It's not so far to Upper West from you." [111]

"Thanks for the invitation, Boris! Very kind. We'll have you over sometime too."

"Be good, guys. See you soon."

"D*avai*, we will. Good luck with..." Mark winked in the direction of the Chava girl.

Strange, but nice guy. G-d bless. Prof Zelig stepped up with a handshake and his knowing nod.

"Mr. Gorelik, we have come quite far. Beautifully done tonight. Great things are coming if you keep this up."

"Professor Zelig, what high praise. Surely, it's undeserved."

"Young man, please go enjoy our evening. Good folks, please let him be." He winked at Mark and left.

Val pinched Mark's elbow. *This would become the rule*, he knew. Limelight was short and woman's patience, shorter. "Two seconds, let me say goodbye to Anna."

Withholding blame, she smiled reluctantly. He saw the fires burning and would tease them.

Mark walked up to the makeshift bar and ordered

---

111 Pleasure meeting you.

Tawny Port. Anna now noticed him, exchanging praises. Emphatically, he would be back, with pleasure. She knew people that he must meet. Mark felt the blood course through his fingertips and toes with glee. This was the start of recognition and great things. The wine's nuance was lost in boyish trepidation—just contained. Here walked up Chava; they were introduced. He offered an idea that she weighed; the mutual regard was clear. Out of the corner of his eye, he saw his jealous Val and begged off with a *keep in touch.*

A wave and kisses to the faithful, he was off. Vova was drunk outside and speaking with a girl—what else, but Dina's type. Mark just suppressed a cringe and pinched his brother's shoulder as he hailed a cab. He grabbed his Val around the waist and pulled her close. He gave the cross streets and they sped away.

A fierce desire swallowed Val and Mark. They barely noticed as they flew uptown, attacking one another with their trembling lips and hands through starts and stops and cursing beeps. Mark threw a twenty and they traipsed upstairs. Val giggled, little girl athrill. She bit her lip and tipped her head aside.

Gathering strength, resistance, Mark took over. Deliberate and slow, he carefully unwrapped what lay in store for him. G-d did exist and smiled on him abundantly. Making a study, he admired her every breath and moan, each hair, inflection, geometric virtue.

Conducting with a keen precision, Mark instilled one layer on another of a yawning expectation. Relenting once, again, a third time, he now left her madly twisting, reaching, calling for him. Almost an afterthought, he took her and possessed her without mercy or regret. No petty vengeance, complex or imbalance pending, she released. The timbre of her expiration arched, cascading in a perfect sequence from replenished lungs.

Relief and justice in the world restored, they coupled for second time. Val settled in his arms and fell asleep in bliss. No comments, no discomfort, power games. Commitment, yes, that's it. Easy as pie. This was the coffin's nail. How could she ever leave after tonight? Let it be as it were.

Mark lay there spent, immobile, but awake. Here was a gorgeous woman in his arms who cleaved to him despite his piggishness. He, Mark Gorelik, a lovemaking champion, was cooked. Not tired—far from it—he'd arrived. He was clear-eyed, despite the wine, at even keel with her, even beginning to detect a proper tenderness toward this woman-kid. She was his match. He had a lot to learn about her, still. If she would have him, he could make her happy, time to time. He kissed her crown. Val hugged him tighter and purred back to sleep.

Now *that* was settled. What of Edouard? A dissident and luminary—not just swine—philandering and leaving orphans, in effect. How grand! A first among his equal hypocrites, so clever. In any case, who cared? His academic efforts to resist were all in vain, the thesis flawed, the execution quite impossible. Yet on the other hand, there was the desperation in his voice—penance of the condemned. Why now, G-d, why all this? Had it not been enough to suffer all of that? To curse him off, excise, forget, rinse and repeat until adulthood? The shmuck just *had* to surface now, when needed like a hobby horse, a fucking cowbell for a rabbit. Bastard. So was he dying or was this a shtick?

Mark turned his head toward the mirror up ahead. Despite the dim light of the corner lamp, he saw himself quite clearly. There was the mark of Edouard, the cleft, presumptuous, the squarish jaw, the orbits sunken, overwrought, the dark blond wavy crown. For someone barely knowing his birth father, he was tagged. The Fuck-and-Run Technique, effective! Piece of shit.

What did he want? Forgiveness? Easy absolution? There was no ticket he would punch, no Sir. No validation, nor high-minded, new-age Kumbaya, let's-all-be-friends. His whole identity had formed around rejection of the evil father, presence null and void. One couldn't just… reorganize the world around warm feelings on an empty place. And even so, *warm feelings*? Pure betrayal. Why would he want Yablonskiy's "care," belated, cheap concern? What, 'cuz he needed the approval of a father figure? Thanks, but he had been immunized. The first of creeping male concern and he'd be at it with a smiling hatchet. *All good here. Thanks, bye-bye.*

And anyway, what if? What if they reconciled somehow? They would be foreign beings together in a room of language papered with a sentiment. The old man wouldn't get his prose. He'd disapprove, knee-jerk, of his profession, "not a scientist!" Just with more force than Mom, compounded by a hardened age.

G-d help him, Mark, nostalgic shit. He couldn't help but wonder, despite everything. What would his father tell him? "I'm so proud?" "Good job, Malish?" "Don't go and make all my mistakes?" "You want to be a dissident with me?" Mark chortled, swallowing a bitter bolus. At least he was a "man of substance," Mama always said.

Сволочь. Ну ладно, черт с ним. Все таки отец. Поговорю.[112] World-weary with one breath, night suddenly caught up. The son of man was felled by mortal sleep. He'd rise again with miracle or luck.

---

112 Son of a bitch. Alright, well, hell with him, he *is* our father. I will talk to him.

# 4

# Alla

"Hey babe. I'm really sorry, I'll be home by ten."

"Uh-huh. I know, you have a deal, have to work through it, blah blah blah."

"Hey, listen, I agree with you. But now what? Can't just leave."

"Babe, listen, we don't need to do this dance. I'm tired, as well, have to cook dinner, then clean up and put the boys to bed. Manuela said she's quitting in two weeks. I flipped. What are we gonna do? It's just so effing hard to find a good one in these parts." She paused, upset.

"Take a deep breath, relax. We'll manage, make some calls."

"You mean, I'll manage, I'll make calls? Ari, I'm tired of your shit. I barely see you anymore, just for myself. Didn't you say you'll find a way, less hours, let's spend time together?" *G-d, she was sounding like a jealous, clinging wife. How sad*, she thought, *it's not your style at all.*

"You're right."

"Of course I'm right. I'm always fucking right. I'm tired of hearing it, ok?"

"Al, listen, this is bad, I know. I'm really sorry, there's not much to say. I'll mention it to Stuart, not to staff me with these hours anymore."

"How many times I've heard you say that! Nothing changes. Can't deal with this right now. Why don't you have your shitty Seamless dinner with your buddies, think about your family. And when you're home, don't bother me—I'll be asleep. In fact, just take the couch."

She pressed End, throwing the device across the table, on the couch. How could this happen, and to her, of all? The strong, indomitable Alla, Bearer of No Shit, was reeling. She let the phone vibrate—once, twice, three times. Черт с ним. [113] She couldn't, anymore.

Some fucking dream life… townhouse in posh Brooklyn Heights! Best schools, plain gorgeous furniture and clothes, for what? They could afford to travel anywhere, but always on a leash. His big break, finally—Apollo. She pushed and pushed him, too, all that complaining—go, make more!

Bitter desserts. You push a man enough—as only woman can—and he repays by chasing the green skirt. To think—she pulled him straight from Loser Hell, now fifteen years ago, with tough love therapy and turned him into superstar. All that, for what? To feel like jilted wife, barefoot, next to a broken tub? This was impossible, surreal. He wasn't even cheating on her—far as she could tell. Herself, she'd

---

113 To hell with him.

come close once or twice at work. Ari was underwhelming her since Tom was born. He'd let himself grow plump and happy with his lot. She hadn't stopped him, either. The boys had taken all her will and discipline; the husband was a willing witness.

Alla teared up. Her sobs were stifled, fearful that the boys would hear. *Why her*? Had she not had enough in life? No father, then to be a second mother—even to her own—to work like hell to make ends meet, to work through college, then to raise two kids while working. There was the burden of her clueless mother; Mark, dreamer with no common sense. For many years, he'd spent and spent, well beyond means, then one day woke up screaming help. She'd helped him out, but weaned him quickly off. Tough love, how else? Was it her time, then now to suffer through her own?

Far from the first time, she now thought of leaving with the kids. She'd manage fine, put kids in daycare, work and supplement with half from Ari. A friend from college—Brenda—was a kick-ass lawyer; she would help. She could resettle and start over. JDate, match.com. She was still youngish, not bad looking, blonde, with manners when required and brilliant taste. Surely, some youngish divorcé would scoop her up before too long.

She was delirious and knew it. What, she would break up family like that? Come on. After the silent, screaming hell they went through in their childhood? Not so fast. But this was different. And *how*? Divorce was just the same, at root. Resources, independence were just curtains for the children's pain, resentment. Her own relentless nature and her strength were products of her hate for father, and her spite. Of course, by this point, what was left to count? The bastard was alive still, even kicking famously. He even had the gall to contact her by email, just the week before. A life-end burst of guilt or maybe politics required it.

The loathsome "conscience of the opposition" was a fraud, she knew too well. But still, he was alive and with another family, a walking sore reminder of the worst of times. She wouldn't even think a moment of a visit or to let him see the boys. Too much of tears and bitterness had flowed to let this luxury proceed. And even if she spoke with him, what would she say? *I hate you, asshole, die? How dare you?* What's the use? She'd wasted much too much of mental energy on him, for years. A minute more, he deserved not.

Anyway, why these thoughts of father? This was not the point. Ari was different, this was sure. He did show up to read to them and teach them lots of things and play—whenever he could get away from work. His family was whole, at least—just barely, with their temperaments, but still. These guys were pushy, rude—especially his Mom—but all the same, they had their Shabbat dinners every Friday, seders every year, even the Sukkot booth the father built each time. For all their sharp exchanges with Penina, one thing was *beyond*—the food. The recipes had trickled down quite well. Tommy and Charlie were big fans.

Alla was tired. She'd given Ari room—go work—then hinted, then was firm. Twice, three times, nothing doing. He was in the wrong. And yet, what did she want? She had her fairy castle and made princes, but her king was derelict.

Patience—yes, patience—this, she no longer had. The law and sympathy were on her side.

"Mom! Can you come?"

She sniffled, wiping tears. She sighed, looking up for direction. Alla was not religious, nearly, but was lost. She blew her nose and yelled back, "Coming! Give me two."

"Come!"

"Be patient. I'll be up."

"No, *now*!"

Детишки [114] never rest. She washed up in the bathroom, wiping off mascara; it had run amok. She rearranged her hair and freshened up. *Can't let them see my state*, she thought.

"Coming, I'm coming! Nu, what is it?"

"Look, Mom, we built a fire engine!"

"Wooow! Good job! I'm proud of you. You too, my Charlie. *Now*, it's time for bed."

"Nooo! I'm not tired!" protested Charles.

"Me too!" yelled Tommy.

"Don't start with me tonight. I'm tired. Go put on your pajamas, put away your toys, then brush your teeth and get in bed. I'll tuck you in and read you a nice story. Got it?"

---

[114] Kiddos

"Yeah, but will Papa come and say good night? He promised he would read to us."

"Papa is still at work. He'll be in very late again. I'll read for you tonight."

"But Papa promised."

"Yeah!"

"Well, not tonight. Maybe tomorrow."

"But he promised!"

"Charlie, you know that Papa has to work to pay for toys for you and our nice house and all the food we eat. You know that, you're a smart boy."

"Yeah, but he has to spend some time with us. He always promises, but then he's always working late."

"You're right. What can we do?"

"Get him another job!"

Alla was slightly shocked. She snickered. *Little smart ass.* 10 years old!

"Alright. Time for pajamas and for bed. First, put your toys away. Come on."

Tommy complained, "I'm tired."

"Me too."

"Me three. Don't make Mama upset. You know the rules."

"But I don't wanna!"

"Цищ!"[115]

"Mom, Mrs. Shechter told us we should ask you about family, like grandmas, grandpas, uncles, aunts." Her older son was clever at avoiding bedtime, just like she had been.

"What do you wanna know?"

"Well, Papa told us all about his family. But yours, we don't know much."

"What do you mean? Babushka told you about growing up, Odessa, then Baku, then Moscow. She told you, I remember, all about her brothers, sisters and how I was born and Uncle Vova, Uncle Marik. What do you want to know?"

"Well, we don't know about our Grandpa, just that he was bad and left the family. But was he tall? And was he smart? When did he die?"

"He didn't die!"

"He didn't?! But I thought you told us!"

"No, no, he is alive."

"But if he's living, then why can't we see him?"

"Well, he's in Russia now. He has another family."

"Oh yeah? So we have other cousins there? I wanna meet them."

---

115 Quiet!

"Um, well, it is not that easy. They live far away."

"But can't we take a plane and go to see them?"

"Yeah, on a plane!"

"Well, maybe, but I told you, it's not easy. He just left us—Babushka and me and Uncle Vova, Uncle Marik. Just like *that*!" She snapped her fingers. "How would you feel if Papa just said bye one day and left?"

"Noooo! Papa wouldn't do that. Never!"

"No! Never!"

"Right, that's because Papa's a good person and he wouldn't do that. But your Grandpa did."

"That's bad! Bad Grandpa!"

"Bad!"

"Look, Charlie, it's not easy. But you have to know. Grandpa is tall and <u>very</u> smart. He is a famous physicist."

"What's that?"

"He studies how things move and change in space."

"Whoa, that's so cool! I wanna know more. Tell me!"

"Yeah, me too!"

"You'll look him up on Wikipedia tomorrow."

"I wanna meet him!"

"Yeah, let's meet him!"

She guffawed. "Well, we'll see. Really can't promise that. It's just not up to me."

"We're gonna meet our Grandpa! Yay! Wait, what's his name, again?"

"Edouard."

"Like Edward?"

"Yeah, basically."

"That's cool. How come it's English and not Russian?"

"That's a good question. I'm not sure." For someone born in Kiev, it was odd. She never thought about it much before.

"So, what's his Hebrew name?"

"Ha! Hebrew name… Imagine in the 40's, Hebrew name in Kiev! His father's name was Samuil."

"That's Samuel, like Shmuel!"

"Sure, Samuel, why not? But Edouard into Hebrew? Not so much. King Edward—that makes sense."

"So what, he never got a Hebrew name, like us? That's weird."

"Not in the Soviet Union. That was normal. Nobody called me *Challa*, k?"

"You're silly, Mom!" The kiddos laughed.

"Mom, did you celebrate the Jewish holidays in Russia?"

"You're funny, Charlie. No, of course not! It was illegal to do anything religious."

"Illegal?!"

"Yeah, illegal. They would arrest you and then send you to Siberia. You got it?"

"That's really scary, Mommy!"

"Yeah. We had some neighbors. The father there got caught giving a class in Hebrew. They sent him to Siberia, to a labor camp. He died there. Just like that. You know that Babushka was fired from her job when she applied to leave to Israel with us? She couldn't work for three-four years, at least before we left. Can you imagine that? We had to live on really nothing. I would help with sewing things to sell and babysitting, anything. Can you imagine doing that? I was eleven-twelve, not really any older than you're now."

Charlie fell silent, picturing this horror. Tommy was thoughtful too, as best a 5 year-old could be. "So Mom, you didn't have to eat all matzah on Passover?"

"Well, actually we had it. Grandpa Simyon would always get it from the Moscow Synagogue. We ate it, but we didn't know for what. Actually, Babushka did take us there a couple times—to synagogue—but it was dangerous, so that was it."

Alla sat back, exhaling. *Mdaaam,* she thought, *what a childhood.* How did they manage all of <u>that</u>, alone, refused, then stranded, then refused again, then immigrants. No streets of gold, exactly, either. The mind could hardly comprehend a woman with three children, no support, able to manage, work like hell for years, pay bills, raise them with culture and with taste. Yeah sure, she—Alla—helped a lot. But really, could she pull that off herself, today?

She had her ever-present issues with her Mom. The endless lecturing, the comments, the all-knowingness, the health tips. Age hadn't mellowed her by much. She was a special woman—yes indeed.

"Alright. One, two, come help me put away your toys."

They followed meekly, tired out, at last. She helped them change into pajamas, peeling off their clothes. They brushed their little teeth with urging and lay down in bed. She tucked them in and read their favorite, "Where The Sidewalk Ends." At nine, she shut the lights and left the night light on for Tommy. She kissed them and patiently tiptoed out, going to wash her face for bed.

She ogled herself closely. Forty was a warning. Her face was slowly getting rounder, hints of crow's feet forming. She dabbed her micellar solution on a cotton pad and scrubbed with diligence. Then, she applied her night cream, lotion on her hands and arms and legs. Mom once used peels from cucumber and olive oil. She counseled Alla, *exercise the face, prevent neck wrinkles and those drooping cheeks.* Hard not to listen. Woman knew her stuff.

Mom had been thirty-three or four when they got out. My G-d. She was already six years past that point. Alla examined evidence. Her breasts were somehow perky still, despite the awful torture—twice—not perky-twenty-five-year-old, but not half bad. Unlike when she and Ari met, she had a proper figure—motherhood had helped. Her arms were not too thick—could use some work.

Whom was she kidding? She'd let herself go, already some years. Complacency and Tommy's fussiness, no treats. Resolving to return to a half-decent shape, she shook her head—love handles, damn it—brushed her teeth and flossed.

The bed was super comfy, but in vain. Alla leaped wildly between two scenarios—billionaire bachelor's yacht bedroom and her fawning husband on a trip to Paris. Away from here, a good first step. No, let him—Ari—prove his dedication, let him show he'll change. A waste of time. No man would change past forty—unless in a Porsche, divorced. *Can't you remember Florence on your honeymoon? And all the little day trips up the Hudson, the proposal, the long nights with Charlie at the hospital? Go find another one like that. But can't you spice things up, dear husband?*

She heard the front door close. He's home. He tiptoed up the stairway. She turned off the light. Ari stopped by the boys' room, gave them kisses and stepped out. She heard his labored breathing outside of the door. He listened for her breath and any sign of movement. Alla lay still, her eyes closed, ready for his entrance. Maybe he'd wake her with a bunch of roses, puppy-eyed apology, G-d knows what cheesiness… Yekh, thank you, no. Fly me to Paris, leave the kids with Mom! Surprise me with some diamonds, something thoughtful, *please!* Do something, loser, don't just stand there!

Ari equivocated. Does one wake a volcano late at night, to talk? He didn't have the strength for this right now. Not after such a long and awful day at work. 43, no spring chicken, anymore. He slinked with his workbag down to the living room.

Alla turned over and began to sob. Why was she cursed with men? First father who could slough her like a skin, then brothers who would never listen, husband who was clueless, with his great degrees. How would her boys turn out, with *these* as background? If Mama's boys like Marik, then there would be trouble; if like Edouard, then they would get ahead, *too* well. If Ari was their template, they'd at least have common sense. Charlie already had his father's temper; Tommy, more the dreamer type. At least there was still time to mold them in her way. Her darlings were still innocent. She'd spare her dark-haired mini-me's and leave them to their own mistakes.

# 5

# Boris

The morning fog weighed like a millstone. His desire was dead. The only comfort was inside the sheets. Once in a blue moon, there were days like this, the life sucked out by overstimulation, dehydrated from the night before. Boris was late, even much more than usual. He swung his feet out from the bed, landing to summon gratitude for his revival, yet again. He took the washing vessel from above the sink, refilled it with a rush of water, splashing hands. Palm down, palm up, palm down. Switch, left hand, one, two, three. He washed while swirling minty mouthful, then relieved himself. Coin in the box for charity. *Thank you, my G-d, accept my prayers and my supplications, please. Thank you for everything.*

He showered quickly, dressed, dug out his lunch from fridge—Greek yogurt, a banana, sandwich, clementines. Spectacles, testicles, watch, then wallet. Off he ran. Ten minutes, he was in the synagogue. *So* late! Kippa on, fringes, then phylacteries. Each had its blessing, then a kiss. More precious than a lover's lips, indeed. Ten men were far ahead of him in service, judging by their mutters, swaying. He raced to catch up, mind still quite full of holes. The order of the words was slurred. The giant with a white beard next to him was in his element, emitting holy words just like a semi-trailer breaking, *Trrrrr.*

G-d help him, he just couldn't focus. Too much movement, mumbling. Sure, he was friendly with these men, but often, they annoyed him. Unlike him, they were born religious, knew this all by heart. He struggled always even to keep up. There was so much to learn! The nuances of *nusach*[116], *minhag*[117], Bava Kama[118], order, timing, coded language. The Kabbalists then added one more layer, the Gaonim[119], Aharonim[120]. *Aaaah*!

Boris was hopelessly behind. He'd only come to be observant in the last few years. On rare occasions, when he fully slept and woke in time to join them from the start, he followed well and finished strong. Most mornings—this one not excepted—he just pattered nervously, alone in his own corner. He was determined not to be a bother. As he prepared to say *Shema*[121], an elder of the place tap-tapped him on the shoulder, then adjusted placement of his head box, without word and kept on with his own. *Demerit, fail,*

---

116 Way of praying (Ashkenazi or Sephardic or Mizrachi)

117 Custom

118 A tractate of Gemara

119 Spiritual leaders of the Jewish community worldwide in the early medieval era

120 leading rabbis and poskim living from roughly the 16th century to the present, and more specifically since the writing of the Shulkhan Arukh in 1563 CE

121 A prayer recited by all observant Jews twice daily, in case of danger, before death and other occasions.

*embarrassment.* Even the simple things were off. How could he hope to make it to their ranks one day, like this?

He'd chosen this; the blame was his alone. After a long and brutal journey, this was it. Boris Gorelik, programmer and Jew. In darker times, it has been "Boris, admin for InsidePorn.com," Boris-Clitoris, Borka Genius Coder, Boris—Ladies' Man, Big Spender. *Oy.* He cringed with every thought of gross transgressions he had made. He'd trampled every law and sense, a bright but stupid kid on *Easy Street*—on Brighton 7$^{th}$, then. He could remember—clear as day—the moment when the cops arrived and busted up their party. He's been *this* close to snorting coke, *this* close to being arrested, thrown in jail. The shock was seismic. He'd left immediately and moved out, resigned, cursed off his brother Tolik—Tolik! *<facepalm>*—and began his life.

Always a smart boy, but not structured, he'd escaped. Stepfather's fists had not been lifted up against him for some time—he'd grown—but staying was impossible. Tolik had brought him out to live with him. Together, they made buck in the skin trade. After the whole ordeal, he started college—Hunter—and moved in on Brighton 2$^{nd}$. With good grades and some luck, he got an internship at Citi, then a job. Now there six years, he'd had time to remake himself. Living on Upper West Side for two years now, he'd progressed by leaps and bounds.

Even as Boris struggled to hold off the brazen, scraggly Brooklyn roots that pushed up at his every turn—now Mama, Tolik, some old flame—Dasha, Natasha, Mila, oh, Regina!—he found the greater hell in fitting with his new milieu. Keeping Shabbat, kashrut was easy—if you shut your ears in company. *What do you do? Where did you go to school? And what's your synagogue? Are you more modern or more orthodox?*

The challenge often was remembering why this, why not East Village or some other rebels' nest. Why live strapped down among neuroses, navel-gazing, bourgeois pettiness, the fulsome children of American decline? He waxed poetic; they were awful. Without a sense of humor or an interest in the world, these randy young professionals revolved between their hopeless dating, boozy benefits and picnics in the Park. To put it simply, theirs were different planets. The men were shadows, pansies, Momma's boys, the poster children for *Come Beat The Jew!* Regard was mutual. When "Boris" would come out, first thing, *drink like a bear and beat the wife, you'd-beat-me-in-a-chess-game-too, caviar-blinis-vodka-oligarch.* Yeah, I would beat you and your smirk right off, you shmuck.

On par, what did he want? This wasn't his domain. The pedigree, the habits, circumstances—frankly, life experience—were much too far removed. Boris had lived three lives already at his 29. The victim stage, libertinage, and then of course, return from hell. What could these little girls and boys pretend to know? Depravity was coveting a shiksa through the window, air-kissing an Italian boy, giggling on second base, a naughty elbow showing. *Oy.* Would that be his result, as well? Not if his pulse remained.

Prodigal sons were all alike. They beat the chest, humiliated, chastened, but not chaste. Life's rain drops would burst out, this way or other, through the pores. G-d knows, forbearance was a bleeding sword. *Courage! Courage!*

His mind now staggered back. The muscle memory of prayer was strong, but complexes yet stronger. He was ashamed to dwell. This was the very baggage he abhorred in others. Why fall prey?

Boris rolled up his implements with patience, solemn and determined to improve. How else but optimism to tolerate himself? The forest of his darkest days was never far from conscience. He bid good day and off to work.

Inside the subway, kippa off, it was all canned sardines. Barely held grimaces, averted eyes shot out at funny angles, not to coincide. Mornings like this, he didn't know to laugh or beat the nearest mongrel to a pulp. Pressed with his back against the door, a rude, defiant lady from uptown in Harlem eyed him like the white boy devil of the world. Now 'twas his turn. Across the car, he spied a looming threat to peace. A dark-haired, tan Mamita, turned away, was simply busting out. Sublime, supine Latina backside in plain view. G-d help him and his primal weakness. He was doomed. Revolted by his all-too-quick, pathetic fall from Divine grace, he squirmed to find another view. Anything but. In front of him, a blonde linebacker in a suit was towering above two ladies chatting in coarse Spanish. There were the usual fellows blasting rap, some other awful clubbing tune. Great way to prime oneself for work! He ground his teeth. Why him? What had he done to earn this special hell?

Outside, he cried release. He rushed through Times Square station, angled like a bull. Into the building, work, relief.

"Good morning, Amitav, Dinesh. Hey Kolya, как дела?" [122]

"Чайку?" [123]

"Да нет, пожалуй. Не хочу. Потом." [124]

Another fine and nerdy Monday morning. What was he doing with these people living in their cello cases? There were so many fascinating things for him—Picasso, Thomas Mann and of course, tango. What had possessed him when he chose this, the Great Guilt or *gelt*? It was respectable, alright, and paid well, but slow death on stilts. Deployments, Agile frameworks, UAT, SDLC. What was the point? More systems for the bank to say it had complied, controlled and mitigated, to emerge to wreak more havoc later? What a trip. Fuck all the reasons he was here. He had to run and not look back, and soon. And yet, the rabbis did say it was bread that fed the soul, no less. But bread for hopeless drudgery? Can't be.

Crestfallen, Boris now resumed his prone position at the terminal. Rivers of Java code, emails, release dates and Excel sheets inundated him. Another stressful week, a critical update due Friday, the full-year review.

Inertia was a smiling enemy. But what instead? Work on a worthless app with hipsters in their Warby Parkers? Too

---

122 How are things?

123 Some tea?

124 No, that's alright. Not now. Maybe later.

ironic; what's the use? No life for months or years in hopes of getting bought? Trouble with equity—it cut both ways. Life was too precious by the moment to relinquish to some passing fad.

He wanted to curse off the world. Why was he always in the hardest spot, between a mortar and its pestle, ground by all to dust for simply sticking to his hard-won principles? He couldn't marry just some girl from Brighton for her breasts and borscht. He wasn't made to shop at NetCost for the hunter's sausages, black caviar and pastries to erase a lifetime's sugar deficit. No question, he enjoyed black bread and *blinchiki*, [125] smoked salmon with good sour cream, *Plombir* [126]and *Mishka Kosolapiy* chocolates [127], but *come on.* The gluttony, the nosiness, the nauseating expertise in all, the coarse conspiracies, the schemes to cheat the system were enough to quit the lot. How they derided faith, the faintest sign, with cynical eye-rolling and pathetic humor! It made one cringe with horror, worse to think he lived and breathed the stench so long.

And yet, no native cesspool was without its charms. The wrinkles were one's own—the anecdotes, as well—then shared complaints and wordless understanding, kids' cartoons and songs. When found among old friends or with a group of thoughtful grown adults, his sentiment's high tide would lift the stone façade for precious moments, guard suspended. And then the toxic comment on "religious

---

125 Russian crepes

126 Russian softserve ice cream in a wrapper

127 A popular Russian chocolate candy with wafers inside, called after Mishka the Clumsy (a bear)

nuts." Alas, the one-and-done. Between the clashing trees, his nest hung on by will alone. He'd made his choice.

After a deep breath to release self-hatred, Boris corralled himself. Not all at once. At ease, you doting weakling. Just be strong.

Mom rang.

"Привет, Мам. Как дела? Как самочувствие?" [128]

"Все хорошо, малыш. Как у тебя?" [129]

"Ну, слава Б-гу, все нормально у меня. Да, ем нормально. Сплю достаточно. Девушки нет. Ищу. Заеду на неделе. Когда там его нет? Uh-huh. Ну ладно, хорошо, в четверг. А Толик как? Не видела неделю? Не волнуйся. В субботу? Не могу, ты знаешь. Опять ты катишь на меня? Шабат! Ты зажигаешь свечи? Нет? Читаешь Тору? Тоже нет? Даже и раз ты не открыла?! Отстань? Дал же тебе подарок! Ладно, давай не будем спорить, Мам."[130]

He bit his lip to blood. Again, the trope, "Don't be fanatical! Won't eat at home on mother's plates?! And just how *can*

---

128 Hey Mom. How are things? How are you feeling?

129 All good, my little one. And you?

130 Well, thank G-d, all is good by me. Yes, I'm eating regularly. Yes, I'm sleeping enough. There is no girl. I'm looking. I'll be over during the week. When is he [Azary] out? Uh-huh. Alright, good—Thursday. And how is Tolik? You haven't seen him for a week? Don't worry. Come over on Saturday? I can't—you know that. Again, you're persecuting me? Shabbat! Are you lighting candles? No? Do you read Torah? Also no? You haven't opened it once. Leave me alone? I gave it to you as a gift! Ok, let's not have an argument, Mom.

you? Is that what Judaism demands? When will you stop this silliness?"

His every vessel popped with anger.

"Как ты можешь? Я не хочу сейчас. Пожалуйста, оставим, ради Б-га! Так обижаешь, не представишь как! Все, *bye. Я не могу. Потом.*" [131]

Boris hung up, enraged. Of course, she hit the place that was most painful—his sincerity. As if his life choice was a fucking whim, the whole thing a G-ddamn rebellion?! He was furious. How *dare* she, with what right? His every muscle clenched. He almost lost it then and there.

The phone rang one more time. *Apology accepted. Let's not fight.* Grinding his teeth, he let it go. They would not change each other more than oil and water, but would always try.

He took a walk outside, cooled down and got to work, at last. After a burst of emails and a check-in with his analysts, Boris was hungry as a beast. His sandwich with him in the cafeteria, he sat to watch the people from a corner in the back. The IT folk were at their most conspicuous, stooped with an awkwardness and lack of grace unfortunately tragicomic. He cringed to say his name at parties, linked with occupation. The butt of endless jokes. "*Boriiiis, kompyutr prog-rem-mer!*" An *IT manager*, a *banker*, neither much improved his prospects. For toxic fun, he offered *steward* or *car service driver*, even *oligarch*. The JAP reactions

---

131 How can you say that? I don't want to keep talking now. Please, let's leave it, for the sake of G-d! You're hurting me so deeply right now, you can't imagine! That's it, bye. I can't. Later.

were a priceless gem, if ultimately symptomatic of his chances. He chortled bitterly and drank a gulp of water. Yes, *one day*.

His pupils narrowed. Could it be? No, way, impossible!

"Lena, it's you?"

"Boris Yablonskiy! Is that you?"

Boy, was he glad he'd taken off his kippa just a moment prior.

"Please join me. I insist." She looked behind her as if weighing an alternative.

"Alright. What brings you here?"

"I *work* here. How 'bout you?"

"Me too. Just joined last week."

"Oh yeah? And which department are you in?"

"Ops Risk. Don't let me guess—IT?"

"*Ba-riiis, ze Rashan prog-rem-mer. Khow can I khelp you*?" he intoned.

She laughed. He ran headlong into the opening.

"Yelena Bogolubova," he shook his head, "ведь сколько лет и сколько зим? [132] It must be five or six, at least. Still living with the 'rents in Sheepshead Bay?"

132 How many years, how many winters? [Often said upon seeing someone for the first time in ages]

"No way, I'm in the City. Upper West."

"Well, hello neighbor. Whereabouts?"

"Low 80s."

"No. Get out I'm right on 84th and Broadway."

"I'm on 82nd." She flashed a smile, surprised. He couldn't help but think, *that's quite convenient.*

"So then it's settled. We must grab a drink to celebrate. Preferably far away from Upper West. I know an awesome place. You've never been there, I guarantee you. Called Lanterna, in the Village."

"Alright, maybe we will, then."

"Great. Listen, I'm sorry. Eat!"

Her eyes were warming up to him. He may have a planted an idea.

Yelena Bogolubova, my G-d. She surely could've had much any man. In high school, she was queen. Queen bitch, as well, but one could certainly look past these things, with age. No ring yet, likely single. Her figure was to kill for, just his type. Real woman with real curves, magnanimous, well-fed on Russian portions in her childhood.

His mind raced to remember what he could from Facebook. Was it Brandeis that she had finished or GW? No, NYU—that's right. Smart cookie. Used to male attention. Travelled to South America, Morocco, Israel. Something about kite surfing, jumping out from planes. Her girlfriends were just like her—buxom, organic, local Russian blondes, all oozing sex, all business without break. *Crack that one, lover boy!* Yes, please!

No, really she was quite the worst prescription for his new condition. *No, no, no.* Exactly his unraveling, the tease to end all teases, his undoing. Yet he had to have her. She had been that unreachable, impossible and undeniable desire's object all the high school long. Much water had passed on under the bridge since then. He had some means and confidence by now. Why in hell not?

There was no future in a tryst like this. Or maybe she could tame her impulse and become observant? Да, если бы... Если бы, да кабы, так во рту-б росли грибы."[133]

*This woman? Much too hot*, he thought, deliberating. *Fuck off, Jiminy Cricket. Off you go.*

He pressed his faculties to service, all at once. He teased her.

"What's a nice girl like you doing in this den of thieves?"

"Who said I'm nice?" she winked.

"Ты посмотри, какая. Так и быть. Alright, bad girl, what is your favorite vice?" [134]

"Wouldn't *you* like to know."

"Let's say I would. We'll save it for our drink. Call you this week?"

---

133 Yes, if only… *If only as you say, then mushrooms will sprout in the mouth.* [Russian saying to convey the folly of hypothetical scenarios]

134 Just look at this! What a [naughty girl]. Well, so be it.

"Why not? Give me your phone. I'll put it in."

The corner of her mouth upturned. Calmly, she gave her digits and then called herself. Boris could tell, she pictured him already in some role or other. Were they even friends, in fact? Was this not scandalous on many levels, much more so, since at work? What had he got himself into, led by his instrument of justice, right into a honey trap? *No turning back now, soldier. Moron.* Wait. He kissed her on the cheek. "We'll be in touch." He winked and walked out with his shoulders high. *You sneaky bastard, how'd you manage that?* He waved his hand right off the stove.

Out of the elevator, he went in for mincha. Out came his kippa, creased. Ten men began their mumble, *Ashrei Yoshvei Beitecha*[135]. By rote, he followed, synapses flooding with an awful lust. With every fiber, he suppressed the Satan. How shameless and embarrassing. He shuddered. *Just think of lowly creatures, roaches, rats, whatever.* The cowbell fever lapsed. Three steps back, then three forward.

Steadying nerves, he bowed and launched into his benedictions. He clenched his teeth three times to staunch reversion and continued. Focus, he couldn't, still. His subdued speech rolling along the tracks, his thoughts unhinged and flew off, far.

*Selach lanu—forgive us. Hatanu—we have sinned.* We haven't sinned quite yet. It is a certainty we will, if given chance. But until then, there's time. Iniquities and sins most grave now floated up like turds, malicious whack-a-moles in vivid detail. Forbidden pictures—worse, positions—compromising all.

135 First words of a prayer repeated three times daily.

*The offhand gestures of a clueless juvenile, shenanigans with damage, binge of lies.* He wanted to excise himself from horrid past, claw back his time and standard from perdition's hole.

He lingered on the blessing for the righteous, pious ones. May they be guarded and protected from above. *Amen!* Once in Jerusalem, he'd seen himself a Chasid in the street with long *peyot*, white hair, a father to a brood of little *tzadikim*, with smiling wife. Maybe this wasn't so impossible, quite still. The dream of *aliyah* felt close and weightless in this space between the earthly labors and the Infinite. One day, for sure—and soon.

Boris held up the prayer book and covered eyes. *G-d, thank you for my everything. Help keep protect Mom, brother Tolik, aunt Rita and her children, Alla, Vova, Marik. Please grant them health and happiness, success and sustenance, everything that they need. Help me, Boruch ben Rina, meet my match, get married and have children, most of all. Thank you for everything, Hashem.*

The service finished and they sat to hear a word of Torah from the guy in Market Risk. He spoke about the story of Tamar, Zerach and Peretz and Yehuda—in relation to Moshiach. *Was Lena playing whore to give him twins? And to redeem the world, as well?* He chuckled to himself. These modern women, damn it, always business.

Back at his desk, Yablonskiy roared to work. Half a day wasted well, he would be leaving early for his date. From every crevice poured more emails, code reviews completed—three!—a couple status updates and a joke told well to Kevin, his new boss. At four, he took his walk, as usual, to vent his brains. Three circles all around the park, enough to chart the plan of action for tonight. Drinks at The Modern, then if things went well, a walk to 56th street on East River. Chances of something were quite slim to none, but standards must be kept. Debora Lévy from the synagogue. What did he know? Lebanese family, born in Paris, then grew up in Mexico. Refined and gorgeous, dark, whip-smart—in school to be a therapist. A lot to like, but such a different flavor from the usual. What did he really know about her? Not too much. What would they talk about? He'd turn on charm offensive, but was that enough? She seemed the type to brush it off, but then she had agreed to come. Oh, what the hell, why not? He'd dated almost every Russian girl there was with any interest in Judaism, with what result? Not much to lose here. If Lebanese or French or Mexican, all for one price, why not?

She was a flirt, this one, but in a charming way. For her, a Russian was exotic too, perhaps. He laughed, a shade too loud. Exotic *Russian!* He was an odd case, it was true, but hardly cause for fascination. One thing he did have plenty was imagination, which ran circles like a rabid greyhound in pursuit of woman and her truths. At ten to six, he ran out, soaked with expectation. Two minutes before showtime, he stood pat, positioned for her entrance through the doors.

Why could he not remember what her face looked like? Only a vague idea—an oval shape, dark wavy hair, warm eyes, a measured smile. Funny thing, memory. He held his bag first on his shoulder and then off, in hand. He leaned against the wall, just so, imagining his body language. *First impressions.*

Outside the door, a cab pulled up. No question, it was her. He straightened up and focused. Wanting to run and open the car door, Boris held his wits and stayed. Stepped out a graceful leg, another on high heels. Black dress, hair up, black purse with silver edge—antique, he thought—she walked up to the door, where Boris readied, opening. Of habit, Debora offered cheek. Seamlessly, despite shock, he leaned in, one, then two. Controlling his delayed reaction, Boris reeled off ten breathless "can't-believes." My G-d, she was a *woman*! *Finally*. Perfumed and made up, she walked in at perfect pitch. His lower jaw was dancing slightly past the choreographer, the eyes dilated with dumb luck.

They sat down at a table in the middle and each smiled. With narrowed eyes, he went to work.

"Ms. Lévy, it's a pleasure, finally, outside the synagogue."

"Indeed, it is."

He now remembered her inflections, so delightful. *Pleasant voice.*

"You told me once a bit about your family. Was it your father or your mom who's Lebanese?"

"My Dad."

"And Mom? She's French or Mexican?"

"Actually neither. She's Romanian. My parents met in Paris, then we moved to Mexico to be with family. Dad's uncles and two brothers settled there, long time ago. They run an import business all together."

"Wow, that's quite something. Romanian and Lebanese! So wait, you grew up with Sephardic customs or with Ashkenaz?"

"Sephardic, definitely, but the other side is strong. My Mom—she taught me everything she knows, and not just how to cook, let's say."

"You'll have to tell me more. That's an amazing mix. And older brothers? Should I be afraid?"

Debora laughed. "If you behave, I tell them, go."

"I might just have to. And how many?"

"Three."

"Oowaa."

The waitress took their order—drinks—*La Vieille Maison* and *Blood and Sand.* To eat, salmon tartare and endive salad and Atlantic cod.

"Old-fashioned, *La Vielle Maison*."

"So Russian, *Blood and Sand* with salmon."

"I guess you eat non-kosher dairy and fish out?"

"I guess you eat, as well."

"One day, maybe I won't. For now, I do. Did you grow up religious?"

"Traditional, I wouldn't say religious. My Mom is not so crazy about kosher, but she keeps the house for Dad. She thinks I'm crazy to become observant, but I want to. I had a rabbi and a rebbetzin in Mexico that taught me Torah, Tanya, some Chassidus, other things. I really like."

*She rolls her R's. How sexy*, Boris thought. *The mannerisms, French*; t*he way of speaking, Spanish. Fascinating.*

"Boris Jablonski, right? Tell me about *your* family."

"Yablonskiy. Close enough. What would you like to know? I have an older brother, Anatoliy. My Mom lives out on Brighton Beach. My brother, too. It's *not* my favorite place, I'll tell you that much. Everyone thinks I've gone completely mental with religion. Can't say we're so traditional. The humor's very Jewish, all the stories—names, for sure. What else?"

"I'm sorry—your father, I mean."

"These things happen."

"What does your mother do? And your stepfather?"

"She is a dentist. She retrained here. Used to be a doctor. Stepfather is an engineer. He works with a developer—in real estate."

"What did your father do?"

"In Russia, he was a clinician. Ear-nose-throat."

"I see. You guys are all so educated. Wow."

"Well, almost all of us. I'm planning to go back to school to get a grad degree. I only have a Bachelors. If I could put together all the online courses, I would have a Ph.D."

"What kind of courses?"

"Everything—art and coding, biz development, some neuroscience and economics, drawing. *Love* to learn."

"That's great. It's rare."

"Don't know 'it's rare,' but thanks. And you, how do you like your program?"

"It's alright. Can't wait to start seeing patients, actually."

"I can imagine, sure. What sorts of people do you treat, I wonder? Is it all neurotic Woody Allen types and JAPs?"

"There is a lot of that, but it's not what I want to do. I focus on young children."

"With disabilities?"

"Sometimes. Speaking of Woody Allen types…"

"No, no, I am a liberated woman, don't you worry." *Wink*.

She laughed—half with him, half about. "I meant religion. How do you want to raise a family, for example?"

He smiled, sincerely pleased. "I'm glad you asked." He scurried to present coherent formulation. "Family purity is key," he blurted out. "It's really everything."

Was he insane? A liar of the crassest sort. His past, what filth! He'd gone through girls like gloves, not long ago, exchanging them at will. Now *this*? Yes, this. That's why. It damn-near ruined him, the cynicism. There was no conquest, challenge, nothing then. They came for money, bling and thrills. Back there, he had a reputation. Here, on another island, he'd rebuilt himself from scratch. Or *almost*, anyway. *Not terribly romantic, talk of mikvahs*[136].

Debora was sincere. She felt the same. *On this, you build a family, a future and all else.*

*Was it a core conviction with her mother's milk*, he thought, *or like for me, a late realization*?

Her smiling and attentive eyes did little to suggest the one or other. And yet, she was a woman, not a girl, he felt. Old jokes about "experience" bobbed up and sank again. *Behave.*

The drinks came finally. Now Boris toasted to their meeting. With the first sip, he knew. The coffee and the bitters were no whiskey, but damn good. They switched, to try. Debora didn't mind and took another sip. They shared without a second thought, old friends. At ease, he stared into her eyes, half-playfully, half not. She leaned in, drawing back at last.

"Debora, you are here how long?"

"New York? Since August of last year. But why?"

"Have you had time to see the city, *really*?"

"Well, I've been here before, of course."

"You've walked the Brooklyn Bridge and been to Brooklyn Heights? You've heard good jazz? Been to the Met?"

---

[136] Jewish ritual baths. [Married, menstruating Jewish women are obligated by Jewish law to immerse themselves monthly before resuming intercourse]

"I'm sad to say, not yet."

"Oh, we must change that soon! So many things to see. I'd love to show you."

"Great!"

"Actually, when we finish here, let's walk to the East River. There is a place I want to show you. *Really* something. You'll enjoy. You can see Queens from there and Brooklyn."

"Sure!"

The food arrived. They barely noticed.

"So do you plan to stay here when you graduate?"

"Depends. I'd like to, but who knows? I could go back to Mexico, as well. The problem here is if you're single, you can stay forever. I give myself a deadline—one year after graduation."

"And you know what you want? What kind of guy, you want to marry?"

"Yes, more or less. He must be strong on family and strong, in general. Someone who wants to have a lot of children. Kind and funny. He doesn't smoke or drink too much." She looked at him askance. "You're Russian. Do you drink a lot?"

Boris could only laugh. She waited for an answer. "Of course! Vodka five times a day. It keeps me fresh and young." He shook his head. "Our reputation is quite awful, Russians. Mostly true, though. Just not in my case. My drink of choice is scotch."

"Oook. That's good. And *you* know what you want?"

"I do," he fudged. Narrowing eyes, he leaned in on his folded arms. "It's simple, really."

"*Really*?"

"Someone who understands me, wants the same things in a family. Shared interests are helpful." His eyes flashed open. And dark and gorgeous really helps. Good cook is nice."

"Demanding man. Does that exist?"

"Well, how's your cooking?"

"I can make some things. Let's see. Boeuf Bourgignon, Mexican meatballs, sambusac, lahmajin. I make a mean shakshuka."

"And you're hired! That's excellent. Let's eat. You've made me really hungry."

"Have I?" They laughed.

"Let's split."

She motioned to him for his plate. "And Boris, do *you* cook?"

"Nothing like this, but yes. Chicken and rice, cholent and salad—basic stuff."

"Bon appétit! Buen provecho!" [137]

"Bon appetit! I am impressed. You speak Spanish *and* French?"

---

[137] Enjoy your meal. [first phrase in French; second in Spanish.]

"Well, no, I wouldn't say that. Just some phrases. Spanish, more than French."

"Maybe you'll learn."

"Maybe you'll teach me."

"Let's see. Maybe."

Debora was a revelation. He was falling. The taste of salmon and of simple salad elevated, splintering to units of pure pleasure. The cod was buttery and flavorful, just right. Boris absorbed his drink, once and for all. *No sense in languishing in soberness*, he thought. *Deceptive strength for just a cocktail.* Had he lost his tolerance?

"Debora, may I ask a question?"

"Sure."

"How do you want to raise your kids? I mean, you want them in yeshiva or in private school or…?"

"My brothers went to Jewish school and college, so yeshiva…? I'm not completely sure. I want them to become professionals, to have a way to live. But Torah is important too. Very much so."

Boris lit up. Balsam to ears! Filled lungs and palpitations, thoughts ran wild. Could she be it? Almighty G-d, could you have sent her? What utter madness. Fantasy! These stories were short-lived, one-sided, usually. But wait. Her smile and body language were receptive. Could she feel the same?

He called the waitress over. "One more round, please."

"So Boris, do you date a lot?"

"What means a lot? Not really, here and there. And you?"

"Don't like the concept—'dating.' In France, it's simple. If you like each other, you're together. Here in the States, they date around. Four, five, whatever at a time. It's so confusing and ridiculous, this JDate system. And then the guys. So awkward and nothing to say. You don't seem so American to me."

His smile was widening with every phrase. A *gift*!

"I'm not American, in many ways. I totally agree with you. I can't stand all the flakiness of people." He was himself to blame for doublespeak, so many times… "You're right, it's not for us, this system."

He tapped his glass. Debora nodded. The second round of drinks arrived. He made a toast to her for being exactly as she was and drank.

Yablonskiy took the leap. Never this early, he now took her hand. Unsure, she gave it.

"Let me see your palm. Let's see here." He examined closely. "You're creative. Smart. Long life line—always good. At least three children, maybe more."

"You really know this stuff. What does it say about my husband? Rich? Good-looking? Kind?"

"For that, I need your other hand."

He cradled it in both of his with tenderness. "He's brilliant, tall, adventurous; not rich –just yet. He'll make you very happy, certainly."

"All that, from three, four lines? Why Boris, you *are* brilliant. And adventurous. I see."

"The rumors are all true." He winked.

"If so, what others are there, Boris?"

Unfazed, but cautious to the point of smiling, he proceeded. "Well, there's the Russian mafia connection, KGB, Mossad. Drink like a horse—I told you—and a chess grandmaster. That and a mathematic genius, naturally."

"And do you beat the wife?"

His smile turned slack with indignation. "Did you just ask me if I *beat the wife*?"

"Hm, yes."

"Just 'cuz I'm Russian, is that why? Oh boy, that's bad. No, absolutely ***not***. That is the last thing I would ever do. Let's just say that I've seen it firsthand and I'd never do it. Stepfather would do that sometimes. You get the point, I think."

"I'm sorry, Boris. Didn't know. I… have some patients—children that have been abused. The stories are so terrible."

"Don't worry, everybody's fine by now."

"That's good, I hope so."

"Well, on a slightly less depressing note… Here's to our meeting and to many more! L'Chaim!"

"L'Chaim!" They drank, looking each other in the eye. He winked. Debora laughed and winked in kind.

"You know, I've never dated Russian guys. You're not so typical, I think."

"I'll take it. Thank you. I've also never dated French or Lebanese or Mexican. It's quite a lovely mix."

They sat like silly fools a moment, ogling each other, hand-in-hand. Something was happening, momentous, cautiously. He sighed. The close calls had been painful torture. Better wait.

"Check, please! I want to show you the river. Let's get going soon?"

"Sure, I would like that. Give me a moment—Ladies' room."

"Of course." He watched her walk away in his peripheral view, still graceful, even after the two drinks. Impressive woman. Most had failed the test.

And Lena, what of her? She was a flirty sex bomb, yes—a glory fuck, quite frankly. *This* was real. For all the familiarity of high school friendship, he had molted, shed a skin or three since then. There would be no return. Too much abuse and pain, misunderstanding and derision, from both sides. *High standards*, right? That was the motto now, alas. In T&A or in himself? One only hoped it was a false dichotomy.

He gave his card to pay. Out of the corner of his eyes, he saw her round the corner, Venus on the Half Shell, dark. What would their children look like? Curly devils with blue eyes? *Shpreching* in Russian and in French, in Hebrew, Spanish, English and whatever else? He'd teach them halakha, as soon as he would learn himself. They would have family—a large one that he never had. He'd take them to museums, teach them formulas, make sure they played piano or the violin. They'd have his knack for numbers and for history, Debora's language skills and empathy for people, temperament and hair. Glorious, fragrant curls, arranged just thusly in a crown.

*Daydreamer, wake!* Debora sat back down and smiled. Her perfume was in bloom. Boris signed off with haste, terribly generous with tip. Guiding her gently through the foyer, Boris offered arm. Debora clasped it tightly. Off into the night they rambled, enchanting muse and charming piper.

Here was a gorgeous public garden, there a waterfall, the best dessert in midtown, gorgeous rebuilt townhouse. And now, the U.N. Mission of Mugabestan. They sat down on a bench inside the cozy park.

"Here, look, you see the ruins? That used to be a mental hospital. And there, behind—can't see it well—a sign for Pepsi Cola. That's all Long Island City there, the tall apartment buildings. That's Citi tower there. I worked for those guys for 6 years until last year. Good riddance, thanks. No thanks.

"What is it that you do, again? You mentioned when we spoke in synagogue. Something computers—programming, I think."

"I'll try explaining it as simply as I can. Let's say the bank needs a new system to control the trading of new instruments. Let's say they want to sell or buy a contract betting that the weather will be warm in late October here. I know, sounds crazy. It's risk management. Alright, let's say we want to buy a contract at a certain price for, say, a million barrels of North Sea Brent Crude—that's petrol, basically—with the idea that it will go up in value by the time the oil is ours. We make the difference or we sell to someone else. We need to track the prices and the contract terms. That's what I build—the systems that we need to track. I have a team—Chinese and Hindu dudes—that code for me. They're called code monkeys—terrible, I know. I get to go design the systems and then oversee the building. Not terribly exciting stuff, alas."

"You like it?"

"Better a human than a monkey, yes." He sighed. "It has its moments, but it's tough sometimes. I'd really like to work with people more, like you. I'm realizing it's just not for me to sit along in front of a computer for 8 hours every day. *Parnassa* [138] is *parnassa*, sure, but what do I accomplish every day? I help the money grow from other money—and for what? Whom am I helping? What's the take-away?"

"I'm sorry, Boris. That is tough. What would you do if not programming, if you had a choice?"

"Great question. Teacher, maybe therapist. A rabbi?"

---

[138] Sustenance or wealth (Hebrew)

Debora mimicked his buffoonish, upraised arms. "You have a teacher's personality, I think. What would you teach?"

"Math, history, computer science, whatever."

"That's nice. You must be good with kids."

His upturned palms went up involuntarily again; hers too. He wagged a finger. She was right behind. He grabbed hers gently, then coaxed out the other four. He kissed her hand and then implored her eyes. Any objection was pro forma, feeble. Her woman's modesty deployed, she readied. Boris took the lead.

He kissed her tenderly, emboldened by the shock of seamlessness. The ripe fruit of her lips was succor to the parched; her hair, a field of poppies. Her features were between Modigliani's *Woman of Algiers* and Ingres's *Princesse de Broglie*. What bliss! Almighty G-d was smiling at him, mightily.

Boris embraced Debora with his being. They lingered in enchanted silence, acclimating. Their eyes and prudent lips spoke rivers without sound. How long… If only… What pure magic... How beautiful, this night!

Their lungs perfused with frightful vigor, slightest movement of the other, each bequeathed a meaning on the faintest sound. If they were mad, the both of them, the better with such company.

After a lull of proven comfort, she sat up and asked. "Boris, how did you come to be religious? Did you grow up that way?"

He sneered. "Not quite, Debora. I'm the 'crazy one.' Everyone in my family imagines that a rabbi charmed my brains out and then cleaned them. It's very much a personal decision."

"Wow, ok. And can I ask what happened?"

His cheeks acquired a creeping warmth. He cursed his fate. *Explain this one, you fuck-up master!* He signed. "You see, my parents were divorced soon after we arrived. Big scandal, then we moved away, then back. Then Mom remarried. And the guy was Russian—in the way you thought. Me and my brother sort of ran away and lived together for a while and worked together also. Yeah, rough times. That's why I wanted some stability in life. The rabbi just turned up. Right place, right time. I got involved. It changed my life. Started with keeping kosher, then Shabbat. It took some time to get to tefillin, et cetera. But here we are."

"That's wonderful. I mean, that you became observant, not the other stuff." She looked at him with knowing sympathy, but not the pity he begrudged so much. *A proper and good therapist*, he thought.

"*Ecoute, Boris, tu sais je tu comprends.*[139] We had a scandal in the family—my father with another woman. He came back. My parents almost got divorced. I think they stayed together really just for us. It's terrible—oh yes—we went through hell, those times. But all the holidays, Shabbat—even with fútbol on TV—that is what saved us. Always with family around and food. It helps a lot."

---

[139] Listen, Boris, I know you understand me.

They sighed together on demand and laughed. He felt the TicTacs in his pocket, offering the box. She took out four—not more, not less.

"Wait, how come four? Is that by chance?"

"I like to have four at a time. Is that ok?"

"More than ok! It's great! Four is my lucky number, Born on 4/04. That's what I always take. What are the odds?"

"Ha, that is funny. 4/04. What sign are you?"

"I'm Aries. How 'bout you?"

"Leo. I'm August 12."

He kissed her deeply from his stupefaction. *It's too much!*

Both fire signs, his type *and* understood him… *What was wrong*? How many times he'd had mirages, *this* in common, *that* a sign. He clamped his teeth. *Calm down.*

The hours had flown like swallows in the night. Past 1 AM! Time to acknowledge governance by physiology and sleep. Reluctantly, they stood, embracing once more with the view. They caught a cab on Sutton Place. Fighting fatigue and lost momentum, Boris pointed out the landmarks of the night. Madison was abandoned at this hour; all the lights were green. Too fast, too soon, too surely, they approached the cross-town passage. He held her tightly. She was his already, in some way. *Was this paternal instinct*, Boris couldn't help but wonder, *or possessiveness?* It was a scared child over-compensating, after all.

He counted out eighteen and paid. They kissed away from streetlights and made plans. Later that week, on Thursday. He would call ahead. Their fingers clasped the other's as they stretched apart. Away, away into the reassuring darkness, Boris launched. No chance to sleep, the hour be damned. Briskly, he ended up on Riverside. The Park was quiet, dew already visible. His shadow scissored in ahead and out below the street lights. The normal paranoia was suspended. He had sewn himself whole-cloth, together with a woman he just met. Caution was silenced by sweet longing, mystery. He held her in his arms precisely with eyes closed, her scent still on his shirt. Tears dribbled. Was this it? Debora, bee. Her voice rang clear as day, leading to shudders in his neck. Those graceful, caring mannerisms, her smile to melt an iceberg, and flirtation, subtle but erotic. Prophetess judge, Debora. As for his decree?

Quite frankly, could he handle her? A woman of this caliber and him? What of his tawdry past? How could he keep pretending, for how long? The punishment pursued him like a shadow government. The millstone of his shame ground down the joy. No, he was fated for a girl like Lena. A tukhes-nakhes devil-that-you-know, with borscht at ready, iron grip on balls. Yes, certainly, who was he to pretend? Big-for-his-breeches, sorry fool. Ванюшка-дурачок, как обнаглел! Держись к своим поближе. Не выпендривайся, Борька. Слушай Маму. [140]

He wanted to beat out the mocking voice with fists. G-d damn it, he had had enough. Not the most learned or the

140 Vanyushka, the Fool, how audacious! Stay close to your own people. Don't blow hot air, Boris. Listen to Mom.

squeaky cleanest, he persisted, simply. His will was steel. He'd make Debora happy, G-d knew only how.

Yes, he'd missed maariv. He was always late. Kissing the door at 3 AM, at home, Boris collapsed. A pounding rain commenced. Life poured on thick. Boruch ben Miloslav Yablonskiy slept the sleep of brave богатыри.[141]

---

141 "Bogatyri" is derived from the plural form of Bogatyr, an Old Slavic word that means "Valiant Champion".

# 6

# Yablonskiy Family

"Ало, Ира? Привет. Рита. Ты как?"[142]

"Рита? Которая?"[143]

"Не узнаешь? Горелик."[144]

"Конечно! Риточка! Привет, родная. Давно не виделись. Как у тебя дела?"[145]

"Да слава Б-гу, вроде ничего, тфу-тфу. Сама ты как? Как малыши?"[146]

"Да знаешь, так себе. Хандрю немного все. Пройдет. А малыши? Одному тридцать-четыре, другому

---

142 Hello, Ira? Hi. This is Rita. How are you?

143 Rita, which?

144 Don't recognize my voice? Gorelick.

145 Of course! Ritochka! How are you, dear? Long time, no see. How are things with you?

146 Thank G-d, not bad, *tfu tfu*. And *you*? How are the boys?

двадцать-девять. Тфу-тфу, нормально, вроде-бы. А что?"[147]

"Да так, давно на слышала от вас. Звоню собственно за чем... Хочу вы пригласить—вас всех—и Толика и Борьку тоже—ко мне на день рождения в следующее воскресение. Была бы рады видеть вас. Мои все дети будут, внуки тоже. Приходите."[148]

"Спасибо, Риточка, за приглашение. Я с удовольствием. Мальчикам скажу. Где вы живете? Я забыла."[149]

"Ист Найнтин Стрит, эвенью Икс. Двадцать-три-шестьдесят Ист Найнтин Стрит, апартмент файв-Ар. В пять вечера."[150]

"Ну хорошо, прийдем, надеюсь. Следующее воскресение, так?"[151]

"Да именно. Давай."[152]

---

147 You know, so-so. A little sick, lately. It'll disappear. The boys? One is 34, the other 29. *Tfu-tfu*, good. Why do you ask?

148 Just asking. Haven't heard from you in a while. Why am I calling, actually? Want to invite you—*all* of you—including Tolik and Borka, too—to my birthday party next Sunday. Would be quite glad to see you all. All my kids will be there, grandkids too. Come!

149 Thank you, Ritochka, for the invitation. I will happily come. I'll tell the boys. Where are you located, again? I forget.

150 East 19th Street, Avenue X. 2360 East 19th street, apt. 5R. Five in the evening.

151 Well, great, we'll be there, hopefully. Thank you. Next Sunday, right?

152 Precisely.

"Увидимся. Пока."[153]

"Сынок, проснись. К нам гости прийдут скоро. Малыш, вставай."[154]

The sprawled-out brute, his balding pate protruding up, let out a groan.

"Вовик, вставай. Ты что? Заснул как боб, в четыре часа дня."[155]

"Ну Мам. Оставь. Leave me alone. I'm tired."[156]

"Malish, why are you tired? What did you do today? Nothing at all. Get up!"

"Nu Mom, come on. I'm not a child, remember?"

"To me, you always will be child. It is my house. Вперед."[157]

She poked, half-tickled him, her middle child. He jumped up and protested. "*Thirty-five*! I'm an adult! It's hard for me right now. Why can't I get a little rest?"

"Ну хватит мне нести. You have to work. It is the only way to keep a normal life. Enough of this. Помоги Мамке."[158]

"I've worked too much for all these years—that is the point!

---

153 See you. Bye.

154 Son, get up. Guests are coming over soon. Little one, get up.

155 Vovik, get up. What's with you? Sprawled out asleep, at 4 PM.

156 Nu Mom, leave me alone.

157 Let's go.

158 Stop spouting nonsense… Help your Mother.

What do you want? College, I worked like hell, then law school, then the firm. I'm tired. I want to rest."

"You are not twenty anymore, my son. You are a father—an adult, you say. A little late to 'find yourself.'"

"But no, that is exactly what I need to do! I can't continue living like a zombie. I'm free now and I need a break."

Rita looked worried, and with reason. Vova had never been like this. Always hard-working, motivated and successful! He was falling apart in front of her.

"Так, ты забыл что у меня сегодня день рождения?"[159]

"Мамочка, нет конечно. Ладно, помогу."[160]

The doorbell rang. *"Go open, please."*

He shuffled in his *tapochki* toward the door, annoyed.

"Who is it?"

"It's your sister."

By undiminished reflex, Vova's ears stood up on end.

"Сейчас, погоди." [161] Bring on the judge's stare. He shuddered, readying his armor.

*"Ey, privet!* Wow, look! You guys grew up, my goodness! Come to Uncle Vova."

---

159 Did you forget it's my birthday today?

160 Mommy, of course no. Alright, I'll help.

161 Just one moment.

He kissed big sister Alla on the cheeks. He felt her probing glance once over at his grizzled face and bald spot, then his shorts and BarBri t-shirt. *Oh, how the mighty first-chair litigator now had fallen!*

"Come in. Sit down. A drink? You guys want Coke?"

"Yeeeaaah!!"

"No, they're not allowed."

"Come on, Mom, we're at Babushka's. Give us a break. Please? Pretty please?"

"Charles, don't start with me. I said no and that's it."

"Listen to Mama, boys." Vova was hedging, sheepishly. "You are your mother's daughter, Al."

She sneered. Mama came out, changed from her housecoat into birthday dress, with jewels.

"Happy Birthday, Babushka!" chanted the boys in unison, and hugged her from both sides. Charlie and Tommy then took flowers from their mother's hands and regaled Babushka.

"Oh, this is so nice, my малыши*!* Спасибо, доченька." [162] They kissed.

"Дай рассмотрю." She now examined Alla closely. "Хорошо выглядишь, тфу-тфу." [163]

---

162 Thank you, my daughter.

163 You're looking good, *tfu-tfu*.

"Спасибо, Мам. Ты тоже! Молодец. New dress?" [164]

"A little something which I found in Loehmann's. So you like?"

"Looks great." She was impressed, despite herself.

"I'm happy that you like. Who wants to come, tell Babushka about their school?"

The boys were thrilled and jumped right next to Grandma on the loveseat. Alla and Vova sat down on the couch.

"Nu, how you doin', Sis? How's Ari?"

"We're good, we're good. Been really busy with the boys and work. Ari's been slaving on a deal for like two months. Gonna be good to go away and rest."

"Oh yeah? Where are you headed?"

"A week in Florence, then Amalfi Coast."

"That's great! I'm sure the boys will love it."

"Eh, they've been to Italy with us already twice. They really wanted Israel, but not this time. That's for Thanksgiving, with the in-laws."

"Ah, ok. We went with Dinka when we got engaged."

"I didn't want to bring it up, but since you mentioned. How's it going?"

He glanced down at his hands. It was too late to show no

---

164 Thanks, Mom. You too. You cut your hair? Well done.

weakness. "What's there to say? It's hard. Much harder than I thought. It's been quite rough on Lyova." *Just dare you, bitch, just say you told me so,* he thought. Finding no words, she gripped his shoulders, nodding. *At least she has the decency.*

"Братик, послушай. [165] You are gonna be just fine. Of course it's rough. These things take time. Just shave your head, already, lose ten pounds, go get a tan, get laid." [153]

He couldn't help but laugh and shook his head. "Always constructive with advice, old Sis. Anything else? Blue pills? A Lamborghini?"

"Whatever floats your boat, my dear. One other thing—the wardrobe. Gotta go. What happened to the fancy shirts and suits? And what's up with the beard? Is that allowed at Weil and Manges or whatever?"

Nothing went past her eye, the witch.

"I took time off."

"Uh-huh. And when you going back?"

"Not sure. I need time for myself."

"Uh-oh. It's mid-life-crisis time."

He smiled sarcastically, his not-quite-dimples filled with censored takedowns. Not with kids around. One of these days, she would receive comeuppance in a bag of excrement, well-wrapped.

"Hey, Vlasic pickle, where is your sense of humor?"

---

[165] Bro, listen.

"In my pants. And yours, Ice Queen?"

*So this was age and wisdom?* They both laughed. The doorbell rang once more.

"Ah, Marik and the girlfriend, probably."

"Fiancée!" Mom had a point.

"Ну ты смотри! Our little bathroom poet, all grown up."[166] She was on fire tonight.

"I hope he knows what he is getting into, Marik," Vlad intoned.

"Come on, sour grapes. He needs to make his own mistakes. Never enough for him."

"Al, you know what? I talked to him last week… He seems to have his shit together, slowly. This Valya's really getting him in shape."

"Детишки, дверь откройте брату! Чего вы там заговорились?"[167]

"Ну ну, посмотрим." Vlad got up and went. "Марик, здорòво! Проходите. Валя, здравствуй. We met at Marik's reading, I believe. Congrats on the engagement, by the way! You guys look good. Come in, already."[168]

---

[166] Well, lookie here!

[167] Kids, open the door for your brother! What are you all hung up about there, chatting?

[168] Nu, nu, we'll see. Marik, hey brother! Come on in, guys! Valya, greetings.

"Мама, привет! Мы здесь."[169]

"Мой Марик маленький, хорошенький." She pinched his cheek. "Вас поздравляю, молодые люди. Mazal Tov!"[170]

"Спасибо, Мам. You look тфу-тфу. Ты молодец. So, happy birthday! These are for you." He gave her a bouquet, deep red and yellow roses, gerbera daisies."[171]

"Ну Марик, ты даешь. Спасибо, мой сынок." She kissed him, lingering to see her handiwork. "Ну Валя, ты готова? Марик не простой у нас."[172]

Val drew away from Alla, who had pounced, meanwhile. "Здравствуйте, *Рита Абрамовна. С днем рождени*ия вас!"[173]

Amused by Valya's accent, Rita switched to English. "Thank you, my dear. I'm very happy for you. Please make me more grandchildren soon."

"Nu Mom, come on. Leave Val alone. We're getting married, isn't that enough for now? Don't worry, we will do our best."

"I know you will, my Marik, but remember, I am not spring chicken anymore."

---

169 Mom, hey! We're here.

170 My Marik, little one, my good boy. Congratuating you, young people. Mazal Tov!

171 Thank you, Mom. You look *tfu-tfu (good, may the evil eye be averted)*. Well done, you're great.

172 Nu Marik, you've outdone yourself. Thank you, my son. Nu Valya, are you ready? Marik is not just any guy/an easy case.

173 Greetings, Rita Abramovna. Happy Birthday to you!

"Oh, nonsense—you look great!" Mark quipped.

"Most definitely, Mom, you do." Vlad followed.

"You do look different—and better, Mom." Alla obliged.

"Ну детки, you are good to me. Спасибо. И счастья вам, здоровья всем." She paused. "Так, девушки, come help me in the kitchen. Ведите себя, парни."[174]

"Да да, конечно, как всегда."[175] Mark sat up close, across from Vlad. "Nu, what's the story, man? You look like hell, quite frankly. Что случилось?"[176]

"Oy, Marik, I don't know. I'm not myself. Don't want to wake up early or to work—at all. It's like I'm always in a cloud, no matter where I go. I miss my little Lyovkin. Even miss Dinka, after everything that happened. I am a fucking mess."

"You don't sound good. What can I do to help?"

"Not much, I think, unfortunately. Thanks, regardless. Mom's done her bit on me. Can't say it's been so pleasant. Just need to get my shit together, back to work, set up the new place, blah blah."

"Yeah, work would help, I bet. But have you gone away, at all?"

"Yeah, went to Vegas—don't tell Mom, ok? Whatever, it's

---

174 Well, kids, you are good to me. Thank you. Wish you happiness and health to all. Alright, girls, come help me in the kitchen. Behave, boys.

175 Yes, yes, of course, as always.

176 What happened?

just stupid shit. Was in Miami for a couple days last week. It's all the same. Don't have the appetite. Too old."

"Come on, you're only 36! Prime of your life! Go have some fun. Enjoy."

"Says Mister-Getting-Married. Please."

"I've had my share of fun, don't worry about me. Plus, Val—she's spicy. Keeps me young." He winked.

"Behave! Down, boy!" They had a laugh.

"Look, Vovkin, I'll be frank. The day we saw you at the reading, I committed…"

"Committed theft? You stole her heart? You were unfaithful? Had an orgy? Steamy."

Mark weighed out one look of cast lead. "Committed, as in to my fiancée."

"You proposed that night?"

"Not quite. I had a… slip of tongue. I said that my intentions were all serious. It kind of just fell out there. Boom. And then, of course, I had to get the ring."

"It's not too late! Still time to call it off."

"Come on, you think this is a joke?"

"You are a funny guy, not always quite on purpose."

"Stop. I'm trying to have a serious conversation here."

"Alright, alright."

"Committed to get married's what I meant." He leaned in further. "I slipped up. I didn't mean to tell her, 'let's get married,' but it just came out, somehow. At first, I thought, you stupid moron, why'd you sell yourself? Just take it back. But then, I saw how she reacted. It just clicked. So many times, I've been in that old trap, but then escaped. This time, I couldn't and just didn't want to. Valka's great. It would be stupid just to let her go. I mean, just look." He pointed with his chin in the direction of the kitchen. The girls erupted in a laugh.

"You guys look good together, that I'll give you. She's a catch. That's not my point. The wedding is the easy part. It's managing the day-to-day that's hellish sometimes, if you let it be. With kids, you get distracted from each other, you forget the fun. The sex is not the same. You love that kid to death, but you feel trapped, you know? Your time to roam and to explore is gone. You've got your job and that's your saving grace. There's never enough time for home, for her. You have to pull your weight at work. Just gotta bill, bill, bill and count each fucking minute there. It's so much stress, you burst. And then, one day, you show up home and see she hates your guts. There's nothing you can do. You hate yourself like nothing else. That's hell. You think, 'ok, this is the bottom.' But it just gets worse. You want your freedom and she yells at you. And you deserve it. Effing shmuck. And then you pull the trigger. You can't stay. You cut and run. But then she pulls you back and slowly, all your guts come out. She takes you for a ride, for all you've got. She <u>is</u> the enemy. You're spent, exhausted. You'll see the kid two weekends in the month, at least. You're free at last, exactly as you wanted. But it's empty, empty as a hollow ball, your fucking freedom. You start to question why you do things, why you wasted all those years."

"Вов, прекрати."[177]

"No, I'm not finished yet. *Keep quiet...* Marik, I fucked it up. What did I do it for? Some fucking whore in Vegas or at work? Maybe for work itself, so I could become a partner sooner?"

"Shhh, Vova. Keep it down. The kids can hear you."

Marik was stunned. Vlad pursed his lips and widened eyes, then nodded. He brought his index finger to his lips. *Keep all this to yourself,* his brows spoke clearly. *Not at the table. Later, we'll discuss.*

The doorbell rang three times. Rita ran out and opened. "Ирочка! Борька! Толик. Проходите. Как приятно видеть вас."[178]

Tolik insisted, "Happy Birthday!" thrusting bouquet of wilting lilies to his aunt-in-law-of-old. Boris was second with his pale red roses. "С днем рождения, Тетя Рита*!*"[179]

"Спасибо, мальчики. Потратились, не надо было."[180]

"Да что вы, Тетя Рита," echoed Tolik. [181]

---

177 Vov, stop it.

178 Irochka! Borka! Tolik. Come on. How nice to see you.

179 Happy Birthday, Aunt Rita!

180 Thanks, boys. You shouldn't have. It's pricy.

181 Not in the least.

"Ребята, все к столу!"[182]

They took their shoes off by the door, greeting their cousins hesitantly, shy. Tolik could feel the weight of his Cain's mark, but persevered. These fancy folks were all alike with their degrees and arrogance—his little bro, no less. Since Mom insisted, he would grin and bear. Not often, he could see his cousins, not at all.

Boris was questioned by his aunt. She saw great things in him, he felt, despite his "peculiarity."

"Borya, it's kosher—*kholodnik?*"

"What is it?"

"It's cold soup. Cucumber, egg, potato, beets."

"Yeah, sure, that's great."

"Ok. Ну, хорошо. And голубцы?"[183]

"Probably not. There's meat, right?"

"Yes."

"Nu, then I can't."

"Жалко. And fish and caviar?"[184]

"Depends which fish, which caviar."

"Nu, salmon, trout, black and red caviar, *sevruga*."

---

182 Guys, all to table!

183 Golubtsi = cabbage leaves stuffed with meat

184 It's a pity.

"Wow, that's amazing!" Eyes flashed wide. "Yes, happily, I'll have some salmon and red caviar."

"Я рада. Вся боялась, чем накормим Борю? Голодным не уйдешь." [185]

"Спасибо, Тетя Рита."

"You are welcome."

There was a knock. "О! Это Миша." [186]

"Misha?!" went the children's chorus.

"Мой сосед." [187]

The siblings glanced each other with an eyebrow raised. Since when was there a neighbor Misha and who was he? This was news.

"Здравствуйте, Миша. Проходите. Вот мои детки—Марик, Вова, Алла. This is Charlie and Tommy. And this is Ira, Borya, Tolik—aunt and cousins. А это Михаил Семенович. Ох, надо-же какие! Wow!" [188] Rita examined the bouquet of gerbera daisies of all colors. "Спасибо. Что-ж мне делать? Аллочка, вазу принеси пожалуйста.

---

185 I'm glad. Was all afraid, what will we feed to Borya? Don't worry, you will not leave hungry.

186 Oh! That is Misha.

187 My neighbor.

188 Greetings, Misha. Come on in. Here are my kids—Marik, Vova, Alla… And this is Mikhail Semyonovich. Oh wow, imagine that, what flowers!

На кухне есть, под раковиной.[189] Come in, I'm sorry. English only, please. Not everybody here speak Russian. Please, come in. You're here." She pointed to her left. "Ира, вы здесь. Tolik and Borya, over there. Sit down." [190]

Rita directed traffic, serving soup with help from Ira. Val brought the Borodinsky bread and sour cream. Alla set up the plates with fish, the jars of caviar, the butter plate. Out came sliced sausages—the hunter's, milk, Moskovskaya. Rita prepared the dressing for the salad, leaving it aside. A well-chilled bottle of Stolichnaya appeared.

Marik and Vlad got up and greeted Misha. Vlad sat across the table, far from Mom, avoiding any untoward attention. Marik—*malish*—sat to her right, Val next to him. Alla with boys was on the other side, warmed up with her imagination, watching. Her little brothers were all grown. Even the *Little Shit* had managed to set up himself in life. It wasn't just the T&A. This Val was good for him, a firm young thing with brains and one strong will. And yes, a figure such as that one, she had had herself. And *now*, there were the stubborn handles, rolls; the spider veins were spreading. Yeah... *Enjoy it while you can, sweet pea.*

"My children and dear guests, please start."

Hunger caught up with fattened refugees. All diets and spare thoughts dissolved. The spread was panacea—close enough. Even poor Boris could no more resist, his G-dly soul outwitted by the animal. The *kholodnik* was magical,

---

189 Thank you. What should I do? Alochka, can you bring a vase, please? There's one in the kitchen, under sink.

190 Ira, you're sitting here.

a childhood memory from another life. Gulp after sip, all three recalled the cold, refreshing pleasures from their summers, mooing compliments. The zone of comfort was aflush.

"Тост имениннице! A toast!" [191] Misha endeared himself. Mark poured a shot for each adult.

"Rita Abramovna, big thank you for inviting me. Your children are so nice. Grandchildren also. Я что хочу сказать... Вы потрясающая женщина!"[192]

"Да ладно вам, всего-лишь суп сготовила." [193]

"Пожалуйста, я не закончил." The siblings checked each other's eyes. *Old fart, upstart!* "Таких детишек вырастили..." [194]

"Мдаа, детишек…" [195] Vlad mumbled under breath.

"Изящна вы, красива и умна. За вас! 120, минимум, вам лет! Здоровья, счастья и удачи!" [196]

The glasses clinked, even as kids suspected what was clear. This Misha was no poet, not the level of Edouard—*at all.* With all his awful warts, their father was *substantial* and respectable. And yet, it seemed that Mom was happy or

---

191 A toast to the birthday girl!

192 What do I want to say? You are an amazing woman!

193 It's not deserved. I just made soup.

194 Please, I haven't finished yet. And such great children, you have raised.

195 Yeah, *children.*

196 You are so graceful, beautiful and smart. To you! 120 minumum, may you have years! Health, happiness and luck!

at least amused. This would be a discussion on its own. Implicitly, the three agreed—Mom would explain herself, if there was something to explain.

"Миша, а вы откуда?" Alla asked. [197]

"Приездом из Ташкента." [198] Now Misha noted the expression of poor Val and the two kids. "We immigrated from Tashkent. My son lives now in California—San Francisco. My wife, five year ago, she die."

"I'm sorry. Must be tough."

"It happens. This is life. What do you do, guys?"

"I'm in marketing. Vlad is a lawyer. Mark's a writer. Valya, what is it you do, exactly?" She straight ignored the cousins.

"Project management. I work in digital. We're also marketing, essentially."

"Oh yeah?! We have to talk." Mark saw his penny stock begin to rise dramatically.

"Very impressive! Mark—what do you write? Романы?" [199]

"Yes, I write novels. Fiction, in general—short stories, a novella."

"In Russian?"

"No, in English. It's my stronger language."

---

[197] Misha, where are you from?

[198] By transit, from Tashkent.

[199] Novels?

"It's pity. I can go buy in bookstore?"

"Not quite yet. I've had short stories published in some magazines before, but my first novel will be out next spring sometime. I hope."

"Вы молодцы все, дети. It's well done! And you?" [200] He upped his chin at Charlie, "What your name?"

"I'm Charles."

"And you?" he glanced at Tom.

"I'm Tommy," he asserted.

"How interesting. So what you want to be when you are big?"

Charlie sat upright, proud. "I want to be Steve Jobs."

"Uhhuh. And you?"

"I want to be a fireman!"

"We're working on that one," clarified Alla, with embarrassment.

"Oh, great."

"Mister, what do you do?"

"I am an engineer. I work for MTA. You know the tunnel for the subway—Second Avenue? I help design it, all the structure work."

---

200 You are all talented, children.

"Whoa, cool!" the boys screamed out, delighted. "Tell us about it!"

Alla and Mark and Vlad all jumped as if to help their mother with the lowly salad. Val, meanwhile, questioned Boris. "Did you go to Midwood High?"

"Yeah, I did. You too?"

"Uhhuh. Boris Yablonskiy, right?"

"Yes, have we met before?"

"I'm pretty sure we did. Remember, at the reading that Mark gave?"

"That's right, we did."

"You know my sister Lena also, right?"

"Which Lena?"

"Bogolubova."

"Ah, Lena. Yes, of course. We work in the same building."

"She mentioned that. Are you in touch?"

"Not really. Why?"

"No reason. But she's great, you know. Real catch."

"Lena is something, that's for sure." With male reluctance, he let out, "I'm seeing someone right now."

"I see. Well, if things change…"

"It's duly noted. Thanks."

"He has an older brother, by the way, who's single. Tolik."

"Oh, alright. Nice meeting you. What do you do?"

"I manage offices for a physicians' group. Also, I run a business of my own. Do web design and advertising, other things."

Boris restrained himself from cringing with an awkward smile. Val read between the lines. "That's great. I'll talk to Lena and get back to you through Mark."

Ira now cleared the plates. The siblings eased their siege of Mother and returned to table, reassured. Misha was not so bad and it was early, still. He did mean well, unlike most other candidates, and there was what to speak about. Tashkent? *Whatever.* He was educated. His son was a big shot in biotech out in San Fran. Not trivial, at all. After some point, they were old farts, the lot of them. At least, there was an ounce of charm.

Round two. They filled up plates, now heaving with sliced fish and bread and butter, all enough to feed a regiment. They passed around the caviar, green salad, also *vinegret*, [201] Israeli dips and Georgian hot sauce, crusty Borodinsky bread.

Mark felt obliged. Vlad poured the vodka. "Mom, I just want to say, you are the best! You taught us all you know and sacrificed pretty much everything to give us food and education and all else. I know I've not been always grateful quite enough. So, simply thank you, happy birthday, may we

---

201 Russian vinaigrette salad, with beets, carrots, potatoes and mayonnaise (with some variations)

bring you even just one tenth the happiness and meaning that you've given us. L'Chaim!"

"Сынок, спасибо."[202] Unable to pronounce another word, Rita choked up.

"Hear hear. L'Chaim from all three of your ungrateful children," Vlad now cut the cheese and drank.

"Да ну тебя, Володька, он же от души."[203]

"Мы тоже, Мам, все от души."[204]

Mark smiled uneasily at Val. *You see, I told you so.*

"Grandma, how old are you?" yelled Tommy.

"Little man! You *never* ask a lady what's her age. Remember that." Mark said.

"Tsh, I'll explain it later," Alla covered.

"Yeah, stupid." Charlie flicked his ear. Tommy hit back.

"Enough! What did I say? We *never* hit each other. Got it?"

"Ya. *He* started it!"

"Nuh-huh, *he* did!"

"Alright, come on." She got up, motioning to living room.

"Boys will be boys," Vlad chuckled, wistful.

---

[202] Thank you, my son.

[203] Ah, leave it be. Volodka, it is from the heart.

[204] We're also from the heart, us all.

"So much for Soviet discipline," Mark quipped.

"They lucky children, but they no behave," Misha felt fit to muse.

"They are good kids, both very smart. Charlie is good in mathematics. Tommy also, very good with languages. Their mother is amazing with them, really. Always to concerts—classical, museums, what you can imagine. She is her mother's daughter," Rita laughed. "А это называется, «сам себя не похвалишь, ходишь как оплеванный.»" [205]

"Oy Mom, come on" groaned Mark. The anecdote had grown threadbare with years.

"Так, Ирочка и Валя, можно попросить вас в кухню? Нужна помощь." [206]

"Sure, let me get the plates first, though."

"Thank you, my dear. Ирочка, проходи. Давно с тобой мы не общались." [207]

Alla returned. The boys were playing with their puzzles quietly. She sat down without thought across from cousins. Now, she wished escape. Before too long, her half-embarrassment, half-shame burst through.

"So… cousin Boris, whatcha up to lately? Last I saw you,

---

205 And this is called, "If you don't praise yourself, you walk around, felling all spat upon."

206 Alright, Irochka and Valya, may I ask for you in the kitchen? I need your help.

207 Irochka, come on through. We haven't properly conversed in a long time.

you were like a teenager with bad acne, all that stuff. You're what, like twenty-six or twenty-seven now?"

"No, twenty-nine."

"Wow, shit, time flies. Pardon my French. You're what, a programmer, I think?"

"Well, sort of. I build systems, but I code, as well."

"Where do you work?"

"Bank of America."

"Oh yeah? That's cool. My husband does some deals with them. He's in PE. You guys should talk."

"That's great, for sure. I'd love to."

"I heard you went religious, too. How come? What happened?"

"*Life* happened," he replied, non-plussed.

"I always wondered the same thing," Tolik broke in. "Right into the deep end." He made a diving gesture, twisting index finger to his temple.

Boris's visceral disgust welled up. "Guys, easy. I promise I won't try converting you. Relax."

"Psh. Good luck with that one, brother. Straight to hell for me."

"Come on."

"Alright, so do you keep kashrut?" Alla refocused.

"Yes, I do. Shabbat, as well. More or less everything."

"So how come you are eating with us? There is a *lot* of very, very not-so-kosher stuff." She cleared her throat.

He bit his lip with indignation, guilt. "I do eat fish and dairy out."

"Ah, gotcha. So you're not really Orthodox."

"Well, yes and no. I'm strict with certain things, but have a sense of humor, too."

"Uh-huh. We're sort of starting to experiment with kosher and with *Shabbos*. The boys are bringing all that stuff from school."

"Oh yeah? That's cool. Which school?" He was relieved.

"Manhattan Day."

"Alright. That's awesome. Glad to hear."

"We're taking baby steps. Don't wanna just fall in. Can't say it was my thing before. Ari—my husband—sort of did stuff growing up. But us, you know."

"Hey, every little bit is good."

"I think you're nuts, bro," broke in Tolik.

"So you've said."

"G-d bless. Just not for me."

Ira brought out the голубцы. The platter was a heaving, steaming tower of pure deliciousness.

"Any regrets?"

"Shut up."

"Ребята, тихо. Помоги мне, Толик."[208]

Boris was the first to help. He steeled his nerves and stomach from the overwhelming smell. This was his lot, to carry burdens voluntarily. That's how true character was built. He clenched his teeth and stopped in front of each and waited. *Fuck my life.* His former aunt-in-law cooked damn amazing things. Now he was sweating from the steam. He grinned and served until the last, brazen-faced Tolik. *Thank you and stay the hell away, dear brother, far away. G-d bless you, not for me to deal.* How sad and bitter, the enormous gulf between them.

Someone described him—Boris—once as hopeful to a fault. Sure, it would be momentous, if one day his brother would grow up. Fat chance. The asshole aspect only hardened since the last time, and the loser manner, too. Was there still hope of change at 34? "Straight to the Devil with you" was his reflex, but he waved it off. "G-d be with him." This was his blood and flesh, all said. For Mom, if not himself.

Vlad asked Misha to pour forth once more. His edgy manner was advanced already, with the family scene. "Mom, let us toast to you. Not least for taming, leaving one, then raising two more wild Yablonskiy men."

Mom's smile immediately darkened. This smelled bad. "Он выпил. Вов, сиди. Please, it's ok. I know you love me. Yes, L'Chaim. Sit."[209]

---

[208] Guys, quiet down. Help me out, Tolik.

[209] He's had a lot to drink. Vov, sit down.

"No, no. I want my toast. Relax." He wouldn't be deterred.

"The four Yablonskiy men here can attest, except for maybe Boris—he's religious—we're born assholes. We're great at courting women, but not keeping them."

"Speak for yourself, dude. I'm Gorelik." Mark shot out.

"Well, Mr. Lover-Writer, teach us loyalty, come on."

"Shut up, you're drunk. We've had enough of your depressive crap. Don't spoil it, don't be selfish."

Vlad made as if to lunge, enraged, but held back, just. Old habits were ingrained, *beat down the little bro for speaking out.* Mark, by his reflex, was quite ready to engage. Mom intervened by standing.

"Хватит пить. Совесть имейте оба."[210]

"Ты права, Мам. I'll take away all my 'depressive shit' and stop annoying you good folks. L'Chaim."[211] He drank with resolution, slammed the shot glass and walked off toward the couch. He dropped himself down without care.

"Вова, вернись." He didn't budge. "Не огорчай меня."[212]

"И так достаточно уже. Оставьте. Не буду портить торжество."[213]

---

210 Enough drinking. Have some decency, both of you.

211 You're right, Mom.

212 Vova, come back… Don't upset me.

213 Already have, enough. Leave it. I won't corrupt the celebration.

"One minute, let me talk to him." Alla got up and went to do diplomacy.

"He's never like this," Mark told Val. "He's really in bad shape." Divorce just really doesn't suit him wel."

"Come on, babe, take it easy on him. Give him space. You know yourself, divorce is hell. He'll come around. But yes, I do agree—not here, not now."

Misha now stirred, encouraged by the hubbub. "You are all cousins?"

Mark assented.

"Your father is Yablonskiy?" he asked Boris.

Ira cut in. "No, it *my maiden* name."

"Ah. But I no understand. Rita, you are Gorelik, right?"

"Yes, it is *my* maiden name. Their father is Yablonskiy, Ira's brother."

"I see. Wait, it is same Yablonskiy, *dissidènt*?"

"Тфу, диссидент. Ira, I'm sorry, but you know… Вдруг спохватился в старости. Весь правый, всех ученых учит." [214] She stopped herself. "Ладно, не будем. Б-г с ним." [215] She waved off.

Mark slipped away. He had an urge to ask.

---

214 Tfu, dissident… Suddenly came to in old age. All righteous, teaching all the learned.

215 Alright, let's not. G-d be with him.

"Вовкин, не дуйся. It gets better, man. You'll be alright. If you need anything—*I mean it*—call me. I'll come out. You need to talk, even just stupid shit, I'm there. Ok?" [216]

Vlad looked up with a laser glance. He breathed a leaden sigh, regained a taste for life and straightened up. His arm grasped Marik's shoulder, then went for his hair.

"Kid, you are alright. Shit happens. Life goes on. I know. It's tough. Some days, it's like—why bother? But then you're right, it's not the place."

"Hey man, don't worry. These things happen. Just don't be morbid. It's not you. You're always running, planning, moving, not like *this.* Do what you always do, man. It just works. Listen, I wanna ask you—both of you. Did… Edouard—*father*—get in touch with you?"

"Yeah, what's that all about? I thought was some sort of prank, the Russian version of Nigerian Prince. Al, how 'bout you?"

She paused. "I talked to him."

"*You talked* to him?! *You*, of all people?" Mark was shocked profoundly.

"Yeah, I know. It was surreal. I saw a Russian number and picked up. Why not? Thought maybe an old friend is calling. *Yeah…*"

"Nu, what did he say?"

---

216 Vovkin, don't stew.

"Well, first I heard his voice. I froze. You know, I always pictured speaking with him, sending him to hell, saying 'you bastard, do you know what happened? You know what awful shit you put us through, you awful waste of space? And look, we turned out so much better without you.' All the best stuff. I froze. He talked and talked and talked. Wow, does he like to hear his voice! A natural politico, our father. Who'd've guessed? So anyway, he's sorry that he never got in touch. He *is* an asshole. Better late than never. Now he's understood some things. Blah blah. He's coming to New York in August to raise funds. I told him, leave and take your wife and kids. They won't let you back in, regardless, or they'll jail you. He said, 'thanks for concern.' So bottom line, he's coming in a couple weeks. He wants to see you guys, as well, but knows you're pissed—you didn't answer him. Look, it's your call. I think I'll meet him, probably. You tell me if you want to join."

"Just what I need, this fucking asshole in my life right now. Maybe he'll teach me how to drop one family and start another. Just like a browser tab, *click click*. Sorry, I'm out. I've made my peace. Don't need a Daddy Dearest by this point."

"Alright. That's that, I guess. Marik—and you?"

Mark rubbed his forehead with his hand—back, forth—and rested, shaking head. *Abandoned son meets father after almost thirty years.* The dream of every breathing writer, this scenario. And right here, on his doorstep, too. Why did it feel a slingshot blessing, this reunion? How did one meet a figure one reviled with every childish fiber, daily, like a real-life villain? With trembling ease, to show one's cardiac largesse? With spitfire cannon, ready to mow down? By nature, Marik wanted to avoid all conflict. But in this case, *too* noble, no? Prudence be damned, this had no precedent. *Of course* he had to see his father, study him and take the disappointment with the wonder. This… *figure* who had sired him, a complicated man? What a revolting luxury to grant. This man who threw off his poor wife and kids, just peeled them like a glove—right off—and galloped back to pasture like a thoroughbred? The thought was sickening, profoundly. Throw in the pompous academic bit, with politics, that was the present's bow.

And yet, perversely, there was fascination. If progeny was such as this, there had to be redemption somewhere in this man. Plus, he was old and maybe sick. At least, one hoped, he wouldn't use the three of them as props for his campaign or raising funds.

Mark shook his head. "Don't see a choice. I have to meet him, see him when he comes. I didn't get a chance to know him much at all. He's kind of just an evil phantom in my mind."

"Kid, you don't have a clue. You don't remember all the shit he put us through. You know what means a woman with three kids, alone in Moscow in the eighties? No, Marik, you don't. Alla and I remember very well. And then, imagine, to get fired for wanting to get out, surviving the harassment and the shortages, no money. And finally, to leave like criminals by night, by train, another train, a third, then Italy.

"Come on, man. I was there."

"Oh please, you were like six."

"No, seven and a half. I do remember, very well."

"You *think* you do. But let me tell you, you were kept away from many things. Poor little virgin eyes and ears."

"Whatever, what's the difference?"

"*Big* difference. Don't start this subject with me. Take my word."

"Alright, bro. As you say."

Mark swallowed arguments. He had his own ideas.

"Should we tell Mom?" Alla put forth.

"You mean you haven't yet?" Vlad was surprised.

"It would upset her. Not today. Maybe after the fact, we'll see."

"*Detishki,* you come back! It's not polite."

"Sorrychki, Mom. We're coming." Mark reassured. "Alright, we'll save the news for later. Come."

The table had been cleared. Dessert was on the way. Ira inquired, "*Чайку?*"[217] Each gladly nodded, stuffed through gills, slinked back. Gastric complaint phased out reward. These feasts were bad, no-good, quite awful, necessary feats, enduring all the diets and foreswearing. This was home and hearth. There would always be cake. *Tsvetayevsky, Napoleòn,* or other long-forbidden delicacy.

---

217 Some tea?

Mom had outdone herself. She brought out homemade and sublime *Tort Praga*, her once-specialty. For children and the faint of heart, there were red plums and strawberries, plus apples. Tea and the chocolate feeling roused the comatose.

Misha was most delighted, praise on verge of overdone. "Рита, вы *так* готовите! Пора вам ресторан открыть. Ну вы воще!"[218]

"Спасибо, Миша. Рада что вам нравиться. Когда-то ведь готовила для трех детей и мужа, все таки, а тут забыла все. Приятно, иногда."[219]

"Well, Mom, I'll tell you this much." Marik let. "Your food is still the best. Don't get me wrong, Val, yours is amazing too. But Mom's is Mom's."

"Marik, *malish moy*, happy that you like."

"My diet's busted totally, but Mom, I have to give it to you. Your food is tops."

"From you, my daughter, it means something—any compliment."

Vova just nodded, patting bulging gut.

"Ты осторожно, пузо в два арбуза."[220]

---

218 Rita, you cook so well! It's time to open restaurant. You are *beyond.*

219 Thank you, Misha. Glad that you like. My youth came back to me there, briefly. I used to cook for these 3 kids and husband, after all. Here, I'd forgotten everything. It's pleasant, time to time.

220 You best be careful, Mr. Watermelon Belly.

*"Mooom!"*

"I mean it. Have not see you go to gym one time this week. You're 36! You have to exercise!"

"Ok, Mom, *ladno*."

Rita wagged her finger and then paused. Thirty-six. My G-d! I can't believe it. We're here for twenty-six. Wow, children, time just fly. Remember when we came in '87, in November? Do you remember what we went through? We stayed with Tetya Sara in Crown Heights until we got our small apartment on… It was on Coney Island Avenue, remember? So dark and small, but nice.

"Mom, can you show the pictures to the boys?"

"Yeah, Grandma, show us pictures!"

"Do you want? One second, I will bring." She brought the albums out from a large bookcase.

Tommy and Charlie were excited. How could it be, they wondered, Mama with the funny hair, red scarf and uniform, so serious, without a smile.

They rearranged around the couch and coffee table for the family ritual, long postponed. The boys sat on their mother's lap, while Grandma opened the decrepit album, bursting at the seams. One, two, three, four fell out in quick succession.

"Who's that?" Charlie was pointing at a picture with a tall and handsome man in suit and winter coat before a clapboard house.

Alla strained eyes torecognize. "That's my Grandpa Abram in Kazakhstan. It must be in the '50s. Mom?"

"Yeah, he was visiting his sister Klara. They stayed in Alma-Ata after the war. Her husband was a great guy, Osip. He built this house you see. We went to visit one time when I was a little girl. It is a beautiful and interesting place. They stayed, their children grew up in Alma-Ata. Don't know what happened with the grandchildren. Mila was oldest, Kostya was the middle, and then Alik. Mila, I think, must be already 80-something. Kostya passed. Alik immigrate to Israel just after us. He's in Ashdod. *This* is my father Abram—Abrasha—he was named. He was a very kind and smart and well-read man. He was an engineer, construction. He built factories—or really helped. They wouldn't let a Jew to run a such big project. It was very hard for him.

"That's cool! Your Dad was building factories? That's awesome, Grandma."

"Yeah, it was. And everybody was respecting him a lot. He helped to everybody. Very kind."

"And Grandma, what about your Mom?"

"She was a lady, very dark and beautiful. Not easy for them always, but they loved each other. They raised us, me and Polya and poor little Vova. He drowned when he was fifteen. What a tragedy! That is why Uncle Vova was name Vova—for his uncle."

"And Uncle Mark was named for who?" Charlie was really interested now.

"Yeah Mom, why Mark? You always told me it was for a distant relative, but I did not believe you/"

Rita equivocated, pinned among her kids and grandkids. "Alright, you're older now, I'll tell you. Mark Levinson—a man I knew before I married Edouard. I was in love, you can't imagine how. He wanted to get married, he proposed, but Mama was against, completely. That was it. He emigrated to Australia, but I always thought about him. We exchanged letters later, but it was too late. When you were born, my Marik, it was clear that there would be divorce. It was a sort of—I don't know—revenge. It was so long ago, all this." She sighed the sigh of ages. "Б-же мой."[221]

"I'm not surprised. That makes more sense. It's a good name." Mark winked. He buried his unease far from the scanning eye, nodding with outward sympathy. His mother had a lover when she married, didn't love his father all that much. And he was bearing the result in perpetuity. Was that why she would smile each time she saw him and repeated *Marik* more than needed? It was an eerie and unsettling burden, suddenly—his name. Even apostle Mark was not this fraught.

He had an urge to wash his face, as if a mask had lifted, residue exposed. He stopped himself—it would be cruel, in principle. Who was he, after all, to judge his mother, martyr of all martyrs, who had suffered first indignity, then outrage, hell of immigration, then the burden of three kids, alone? Had she not sacrificed quite everything for

---

221 My G-d.

them—ungrateful, haughty, over-educated fools? She was a saint, but human nonetheless. The precipice had broken suddenly. One could expect somewhere a moment in adulthood when the scaffolding collapsed, exposing flaws and errors crumbling down. Alla and Vova had long urged him to relent and see the light. Mom was no prophet and was downright wrong sometimes. The thought of "scaling down to size" was a repugnant ruse, concocted by two egomaniacs. But had they been mistaken thoroughly, in all? Or was his ego just more stubborn in its bundled refuge? The truth was flailing in the middle, much as always, but the blow had stung.

Mark leaned back in his chair away from line of sight. Why force this bitter rite of passage down his throat? Why now, of all? It was the time to face harsh truths, apparently. This was the end of childhood. Could it be? The Rock, The Guide, Redeemer, Cornerstone, the youngest soul he knew, Mom was… retiring in five years. His Dynamo was not eternal.

His heart sank to the point of tears. He looked up to prevent the trickle. No one seemed to notice—maybe Val. Why did this simple, banal truth so shake him? Was he mad? The youngest was the most attached to mother, the most sensitive, they said. He was a sentimental fool, that's all. *Cheer up*, he forced himself.

"What's that?" Tommy yelled out. An orange swatch with scribbles, green and faded, was picked up.

"*Rita Gorelik. Malchik.* This is your uncle Marik's band from hospital, when he was born. Here is for Vova, also *malchik.*

*A vot* Alla's." They passed around the relics with great care. All three grew wistful and reflective. Alla remembered seeing first one, with the cutest blondish down, and then the second, with his darkish curls. Alla had made for one stern and tough-loving surrogate for them. She'd been through hell herself, losing a father to some scheming bitch like that, at an exposed fifteen.

"Grandma, who's that?" The boys were on the edge with curiosity.

"That... is your Grandpa Edouard."

"That's him? I want to see. Mom said he ran away and started a new family. He really did that? Is he bad?"

Rita was disappointed with her daughter. "*Children shouldn't hear such things,*" she thought.

"Everyone makes mistakes." Alla broke in. "It happened a long time ago. Already almost thirty years! Bad or not bad, it doesn't matter. He's your grandfather and he wants to meet you."

"But I don't want to meet him," Charlie said. "He's bad."

"Boys, listen. You don't choose your family."

Marik and Vova perked up, trading incredulity. *Who had kidnapped their sister? Who was this?*

Charlie looked up and rolled his head, first left, then right. "But why did Grandpa choose another family?"

"Sometimes you make the wrong decisions when you're

young and silly. Then, when you're older, you can realize that you were wrong."

Alla was feverish, it must be. This was revelation.

"Послушай, он тебе звонил?" Mama suspected what seemed obvious. [222]

"И даже если он звонил, так что? О чем нам говорить? Поезд давно ушел." [223]

"А вам, ребята, он звонил?" [224]

"Ну да, звонил." Vlad let. "Трубку не брал. Зачем мне надо это все?" [225]

Ira appeared uneasy—truly—for the first time now.

"Он меня тоже попросил контакты ваши. У меня нету, так что не дала." [226]

"Детишки, *я* с ним говорила." Rita opened up. [227]

All three were frozen with their saucer eyes. Mom was the one who gave Edouard their phones.

"А что вы так? Давно его простила. Ради Б-га,

---

222 Listen, he called you?

223 And even if he did, then what? What is there to discuss? That train left long ago.

224 And did he call you guys?

225 Yeah, he called… Didn't pick up. Why do I need all this?

226 He also asked me for your contacts. I just don't have them, so I couldn't give them out.

227 Kids, I did speak with him.

встретитесь. Отец, ведь все таки. И внуков приводите. Он здесь будет через месяц-два."[228]

There was a pregnant, leaden pause. What had just happened, a tectonic tremor? What had, exactly, rendered this apocryphal, inscrutable about-face from the granite crag? One didn't know, just then—stand tall, collapse, from laughter or from tears.

---

228 And what's so strange? I asked him, long ago. For G-d's sake, meet him. He *is* your father, after all. And take the grandkids. He'll be here in a month or two.

# 7

# Edouard

Rita awoke perplexingly refreshed. The heavy food and alcohol had kept her up well past her bedtime. How pleasant to have kiddos and their little ones at home, for once! That by itself had added years. She'd dreamt a favorite dream—a chase with suitcases and trains, the little ones with her, Marik in hand with Alka, running, crazy, very late. The train was leaving, just as usual, just within reach. *Why of all nights, last night*? Edouard was waiting patiently and smoking at the station doors. They ran by, eyeing him with languor, but he kept on, calmly, *smiling*! What did this mean? Some sort of vodka residue, must be.

She rose and washed. Her patient, dutiful routine felt somehow forced. Ну, надо меньше пить.[229] She sneered and yawned. Что-то не так.[230] She felt uneasy. Bad digestion? Maybe, maybe not. She dressed and sat at the computer for her morning news. *Syrians dead. Egyptians too. Blah blah Obama. More, same garbage. Time to go. Israel news. Uhhuh. Lieberman interview. Nothing so new or scandalous. Now*

---

229 Gotta drink less. (see footnote 99 for further details)

230 Something's not right.

*Russian. Putin divorces. Cynic SOB. His silent and supine supruga,* [231] *what a sorry plight. Turkmen attacked near to Bolotnaya. The Russian MIT in trouble—what a shock. The only question—who had stolen money? She scanned the front page lazily, by habit. Toward the bottom, something caught her eye.* "Яблонский скончался от приступа."[232]

"Как? Нет, не может быть. Ведь он же молодой. Всего-лишь шестьдесят-два. She read on further. "Диссидент, физик... Б-же Мой! Эдик скончался! Как он смел? Что-ж я скажу детишкам? Они-же так хотели его—видишь, не смотря на все."[233]

With covered mouth, Rita could only shake her head. Poor children, his young sons. For once, she felt a pity for that bitch of bitches, Luda. To have your husband die and leave you like that. What an awful thing! G-d, what a shame. Why now?

She couldn't help but read until the end. They'd picked him up at 2 AM at home, милиция [234] or FSB—same heinous bastards—and had "questioned" him. After three hours, he had had a heart attack. The help was slow in coming—what convenience—and he passed in custody. Full life, but gone like this? She never understood his sudden switch to politics—how could a man of taste? No decency… My G-d, but why right

231 Spouse

232 Yablonskiy has died from a heart attack.

233 What?! How could it be? No, it's impossible. But he's so young. Just 62… Dissident, physicist. My G-d! Edik is dead! How *could* he? What will I tell the kids? They so much wanted just to see him, despite everything.

234 Russian police

now? Maybe they knew he was to fly to States and roughed him up? Not quite a young buck, Edik, but a heart attack…

Rita ashamedly remembered, she had wished him cancer once. Time certainly had healed her with forgiveness, yet the sting of memory remained. The bitch's son had ordered it, no doubt. For what? What danger was there in a bard and physicist, an academic with no business sense?

Why was she grieving? He was not her husband. The bastard left her with three kids, alone. No laughing matter. He was a cynic, not a man—a traitor, all of the above. But he was *something* in a sea of nothings, a real *mind*, well-read, well-versed, could sing and play guitar, wrote poetry and was respected. Where did one find such men today? Mostly long dead, together with her youth. Entire language, context, sensibility were gone, hiding in corners in old flats in Moscow, long collecting dust. Yes, they had theater, arts and music, certainly—perhaps much better even, now. And yet, the dread itself was different from the Soviet time. It was a rot born of self-pity, not a willful ignorance. Who cared much, anyway, these days?

Rita looked up. Her phone was ringing without end. Marik and Vladik, even Alka called. They must have read. О Б-же. Батьку потеряли дважды, детки. Бедные мои. [235]

*How does one lose a father twice?* she thought. *How cruel. No more, no less than resurrecting gymnasts. Let them rest.*

## *The End*

[235] Oh G-d. They've lost their Daddy twice, poor kids of mine.

# About the Author

Yuri Kruman was born in Moscow and moved to Kentucky at nine, where he grew up. He studied neuroscience and anthropology at UPenn before receiving his law degree. He has worked on Wall Street and in healthcare. He lives with his wife and daughter in Manhattan. Yuri's first novel, "Returns and Exchanges," was published by Author House in 2013.

www.ingramcontent.com/pod-product-compliance
Ingram Content Group UK Ltd.
Pitfield, Milton Keynes, MK11 3LW, UK
UKHW040015200726
13854UKWH00001B/207

9 781491 847763